Stuck In an Elevator Between the 12th & 14th Floors of an Apartment Building on Rossmore

a Novelby Morgan Drolet

NEON BURRITO PUBLISHING
 SEVEN

There may be misquotes or misinformation. If so, I'd like to take no personal responsibility. Thanks ;)

Cover design/photo by Morgan Drolet
For more stuff visit: morgandrolet.com
OR
NeonBurrito.info

Originally published by Neon Burrito Publishing, July 2016
ISBN: 978-0692747742
ISBN-13: 0692747745

I want to live alone in the desert
I want to be like Georgia O'Keefe
I want to live on the Upper East Side
And never go down in the street

Splendid Isolation
I don't need no one
Splendid Isolation

Michael Jackson in Disneyland
Don't have to share it with nobody else
Lock the gates, Goofy, take my hand
And lead me through the World of Self

Splendid Isolation
I don't need no one
Splendid Isolation

Don't want to wake up with no one beside me
Don't want to take up with nobody new
Don't want nobody coming by without calling first
Don't want nothing to do with you

I'm putting tinfoil up on the windows
Lying down in the dark to dream
I don't want to see their faces
I don't want to hear them scream

Splendid Isolation
I don't need no one
Splendid Isolation

-Warren Zevon
Splendid Isolation

One cannot dwell on these things, these echoes of what might, in some other age, and in some other body, have been; one must attempt to deal with what is, or else go under, or go mad. And yet- to deal with what is! Who can do it? I know that I could not. And yet I knew that I had to try.

-James Baldwin
tell me how long the train's been gone

This story isn't about alcoholism. It's just about some things.

Here's to you
Los Angeles

3:00 am. A car points it's dim headlights down the exit at Silverlake Blvd. Turning left onto Beverly, breifly illuminating the red and green sign marking a cantina. Below the overpass, a bike is passed over a dilapidated chainlink fence, hurry the fuck up, someone directs from the shadows. The car signals with beating blinker and the Western Exterminator Man shrinks in the rearview. Gas stations, bus stops, technical schools flash by. The pawnshop across from the Vermont/Beverly redline terminal, unwavering in it's constant ped-dling of neon cash exchange. Kitty-corner from the Jollibee, where they serve the spaghetti with chunks of hotdog, burgerYum & chick-enJoy- through the window in a sixth floor corner apartment at the Dicksboro, he watches it cruise, slipping auburn radiance through iridescent predawn.

The blinds sigh plastic snap relief as he steps from his perch, beginning slowly, circling the four corners of the room. Barefoot; Heel ^ toe, heel ^ toe. Sitting butterfly position in the middle of the thinly carpeted room until his feet begin to tingle. Lay back. Tens-ing every muscle in his body, picturing the palm trees; looming bent taut with their engorged heads, a snapshot line of withered men boarding a sunrise bus. As the muscles release, a shutter rakes slowly through his extremities upward, head shaking and he's still. Concen-trate on the tense blades of carpet as they slowly weave their imprint grooves in his back. Eyes closed, picturing each dirty coarse woven hair dimpling the flesh, bending beneath his weight, tickling the face of the fez wearing monkey tattooed on his left shoulder blade. He will lay here till his skin begins to twitch with fury, move to the bed he thinks, but wonders how long he can keep his actions dead to his wants.

It has been too long since he's felt something firm. Some-thing solid. Anything with weight, foundation, an object or notion to be sure of, tethering him to reality, or, at least, any kind of reality he can see himself surviving. Clenching eyes tight, relaxing, he searches for an emotion that can force him to weep. Staying loose and waiting for the melancholy to kick in, listening for the city, for the noises that make him feel so small and at the same time so big, so a part of the grinding mechanism of Los Angeles, part of the maddening turnstile of metropolitan history, so alone in a lonely studio, trying to conjure tears for a fix, some emotional release, a cleansing.

There is nothing better than the vast calm desolation that comes at the end of a solitary weeping purge. How spent, how relaxed the shoulder muscles, how perfectly empty of light and shadow for an instant. Wanting nothing but to revel in a clean slate, void and fresh, till that moment passes and stimuli begin to build again. But right now he can't cry. Can't even lapse into that familiar state of beautiful sorrow that seems to seek him out at a whim. Now, when he wants it, it's elusive, cagey.

Living with constant ventilation is nice for people with windows but, even on the sixth floor, the dust and dirt and asphalt, beat to a fine powder, settle and cling to the frame, the blinds, counter tops, lungs. Ceiling fan blades shake gently, collecting experimental levels of debris. He is fishing through the oil pocked dregs of cold minestrone soup from a can. A siren wails, leaving a heavy cloud to linger and sink, adding production value to the foot fall shadows that patter past the lighted slit beneath his door.

This is how he had dreamed of adult life. The life of a bohemian. At least in some ways. Looking back at childhood, or, his teenage years; whenever that time is when you start forming the, hopefully, unique moral and idealogical manifesto that will be the fiber of your future goings on, he can remember vague ideas of what he would have called goals or dreams. There are memories of wanting to be this or that, do this or that, be perceived a certain way. It seems more like he'd had ideas of how he hoped to feel as an adult, maybe based on the way it looked like adults felt, maybe based on the fact that adults seemed so sure of what was going on. So the child that was he, had visions for a future of a contrary nature. Visions of a timeless, calendar-less, grand vagabond life, eating soup on dingy floors, of whiskey breakfast, of ambling conversation on philosophy and sharp jackets brimming with pills or stories.

In the effervescent, tactile characters of Steinbeck's tramps he'd found a blueprint, but had never imagined the complexities, the curve balls, the innumerable actions and counter-actions of life. Never realized that inaction also has its fallout. Looking down at twinkling starlight Hollywood he feels a surge of helplessness, of power, the unity and distinct separation of countless hopeful souls traversing the same lost highways and byways, each one for the first time every time, never knowing what comes next or when.

He has the dingy floor and the soup. The whiskey break-fasts and jackets and stories and pills. Now he needs the human props of his bohemian dream. A woman. A woman, or series of women, who understand how to share the nights spilling into mornings, the lazy booze thatched afternoons. And people. He and the woman will exist in the ebb & flow of bodies. Diverse in look, class and creed, varied in interest and pursuit, but real, raw, working-man type folks. They will cook fine meals of greasy chickens and vegetables blaring with aroma. There will be aperitifs & digestifs and booze in colors & shapes & sizes. There will never not be music playing and people talking about things that matter. Wanting all the people from all the different places to trip into his world and he into theirs.

But the number of people he knows is none. None in LA at least. And not so many elsewhere. Some have told him flat out that his drinking is too much to tango with, that they can no longer bear him and his burden. Others have simply dropped off. Likely for the same reason. He is a liability to himself and others. Has been for some time now. Wishing he could be rid of the drinking and his current self but the only way to be rid of the he he cannot face is through the drinking. Anyway, people have dropped off. But this is a new day. A new city. And the people here are different. Have to be. They come here looking for things, find things, or keep looking. Drive, fly, walk or swim to be here, where things are happening. He just has to plant himself in places where other cacti blossom. Haunt-ing old movie theaters, warming chairs in bookstore poetry readings, wandering under the diffused lights at gallery openings, be loose of tongue in dimly lit corners of afternoon bars. People will see him, as he sees himself, they will be drawn to him, his truth. They will say to each other: There is an artist, uncompromising, grounded, full of spirit and rife with the experience of life. Let's go talk to him. He'll be up to his ears in stories, asses to elbows with creative juggernauts gulping deep breaths of the city, thriving on smog, flourishing at night… But right now he still has to find those folks.

Ride, jostle, shimmy, the Red Line to Hollywood/Highland, wandering in one bar and out the other. Headed east. At each he is the sole occupant of a stool. If he didn't have two elbows on the bar, one would have died of loneliness. Passing the time of a drink with one disinterested bar tender and the next. Where are the gamblers with their track books covered in pencil scratch and eraser ghosts making heated bookie calls?, the painters sketching the congregants of the local watering hole?, the poets raising glass after glass to plumb their souls and eulogize the day?

At the Frolic Room chasing one double with another before dripping back into the rushing mechanism of the boulevard. Heading down Cahuenga toward Amoeba with the intention of chatting up some spindly connoisseur in the jazz section, or some green mohawk sporting chick flipping through punk records. He will connect with the outlying elements. Gain entrée to some thus far unknown-to-him underground. He will finish this day, not as it had started, alone, but instead, owner of a promising road map routed with trails on which to embark.

Crossing the threshold, blindsided by the force of a thousand people milling, the drone of commerce, the click-clack-ding of cash registers and a muffled voice crackling over the intercom. Wandering the isles half-heartedly, doing one lap and bypassing the movie section upstairs, before exiting without speaking word one.

What the hell was he thinking? What would he have said to some stranger in a record store? I see you have Coltrane. Where could a guy like me find the underground artistic elements that will fill some deep longing abyss of the soul, until now dulled by alcoholism? How do you make friends or even acquaintances in your late twenties? He'd never had much success as a youth. Never developed that skill. Every friend he's ever had had been introduced by someone he already knew, who'd been introduced by someone he already knew, tracing back in lineage to someone he'd been sat next to in the 3rd grade. All the women in his life were friends of friends, co-workers, or neighbors. He can be decent at meeting people in forced proximity. And even then it takes most people a while to warm to him. Longer, if ever, to find some understanding.

Walking into Bogies Liquor, thinking that the 70's were a time to live in. A time to pick up stakes & become whatever you saw yourself as. When you *could* live on dreams for cheap in squats or tenements or out in the wilderness. When you could live in a tent off the back of a motorcycle. When you could taste the validity of the world in early morning/late night coffee, in thick maple syrup, the grit of the streets riding on the wind.

But then, people still do these things. Still manifest their shaggy dreams & ride foreign soil on motorcycles kicking dust & bounding over potholes. How? How can he even imagine a reality so different than the one he finds himself in? He should have been dead by now. Or rich. These being the best and most likely outcomes of any real plans he'd ever made. Instead he sits facing a present, a future, where he will have to work toward goals. Will have to make goals, and then work toward them. Then make new goals & work toward those. Constantly vigilant, course correcting & learning from missteps, creating and taking advantage of opportunities. He's always known no one would give him anything. But he'd never bothered to realize that, since they wouldn't, the responsibility would land on him.

Sometimes it takes a lot of work to turn off the bullshit and face the day. Over the years he's managed to turn everything into a coping mechanism; coffee, booze, women, friends, art, music tv books movies food drugs staring into space. Anything to take his mind off the immediate, the future or the past. Anything to keep from facing the vague indecipherable decision filled paths of life. If Robert Frost is to be trusted, the choosing of a path will make all the difference. So too then can the choosing of the wrong path. And so, Paul Trune runs from the entrances of paths. Or stands debating them. Or choses one, foolishly, with only the vague consideration of a drunk, coming to, somewhere down the road to wonder how he's gotten here.

A crowd has gathered outside the house in anticipation. A milkman on a bicycle with hands made of grape juice, a middle aged puerto rican pool boy with a thick graying mustache, black short shorts with silver trim and a white chefs coat hanging out the bottom of a gold cumber bun, two old women on horseback head to toe shattered with fake diamonds in moth eaten grey and olive colored gowns their hats cocked remonstratively and curling toward eggplant skies. The lights are on now and the pool boy leans in, while double checking his arrangement, for a better look. The rest of the group muttering and murmuring No one can remember how they got here or why, but we're all curious and the late night teal shimmer glow white of the pool combs our bodies. Any moment now. The air molecules zip toward a heated frenzy in anticipation, generating little rippling sparks that pop silently blistering the tension. A woman walks out the sliding glass door wearing a coarse striped sweater and tight black leggings, shoeless and without a hair on her head. Blank pale rolling hills once adorned with now absent eyebrows. Disrobing she stands with perfect posture, gently hanging her clothes from a thick wooden fence near the edge of the water. Her entire body devoid of hair, flickering in the hollow tungsten glow. The petite figure is triumphant and inspiring and sad. Some blue rectangle stillness of the pool glistens, burning in her far away gaze like a projector light too close to the film. We can all feel the weight of emptiness, the fear vacuum inside our stomachs. The painful awe. As she begins to speak we hold our breath collectively.

Looking at the mirror. At himself looking at himself. People have commented on his average height, but he feels short. 5'8" on a good day, his dad would say. 150 lbs. maybe. More or less. He doesn't own a scale, and his visits to the doctor have been infrequent in recent years. He has brown hair, slicked back with Murray's, tattoos with no meaning, glasses, a beard, all components to be mistaken for a hipster. Maybe not even mistaken. Fine. Just another point to put on the list of things to be accepted and moved on from. It is a long list. Getting only longer. With clothes on, he looks to be in reasonably good shape, but is probably not. Skin the color of aged paper. But not like jaundice. Just kinda aged white, but, steadily marching toward jaundice. But really white in the generally unexposed parts.

But who is he really? Searching for himself in the mirror. He wants to be alone, mostly. Doesn't know how to be for too long. Doesn't know how to be not alone for too long either. Seeking friends & lovers, new relationships, only to be disappointed, to leave them behind without goodbye. Fade out, him or them, eventually. He gets rid of phone numbers, addresses, memories. Thinks now he must find happiness in himself, now again in someone else. In love. And when he loses these connections, he wonders whether they are worth the Continued Search. Does he want to create a potentially forever recurring theme of seeking and disappointment, finding & loss? Does he have the energy? How deep is the well of self sabotage? Does he even have the wherewithal, is it possible to stand and deliver himself to the world without jokes or masks, without defining the audience and playing to its every situation?

Maybe if he does one honest thing a day, that's enough. One pure thing. Something to hold up to a standard and say, Yes, that will do. One thing that's captured in it's full honesty in an instant. Leaving the body washed and spent. The wearing down of a pinched nerve.

But how to live honestly in a world where egos and emotions run rampant? How to exist. Without motive for gain or out of fear of loss, fear of missing out, FEAR. He doesn't know. Doesn't know. So he combs his hair and brushes his teeth, tries to remember to stand up straight. A passable illusion of life, ready to mingle and molest another day.

Walking on splinters of sand and gravel, over thin cracks delineating the tiny islands of terra firma, I can hear the displaced grains fall into these fine chasms at the shuffling of my feet. Listening for the far away shudder of them finally reaching the sea of empty floating heat below. The large oaks, so black/purple and endless; smoke puffs violently out of chimney sweep leaves into a vermillion checkered sky, warped like over-lapping layers of a translucent clingfilm fish bowl. Large piles of tiny colored birthday candles, swirling barbershop poles melt together at the edges of the road, upward mingling with the smoke in delicate streams of undulating sexual caress. I walk forward, only able to feel the weight of gravity on my body through the impact of heels to earth, sending a compression wave like a slingshot up the flesh, the weight of which sluggishly fights back the collision. Now my vision is dappled with nearly suspended droplets of immersive warmth like a rain of black ghost oil falling slowly, much slower than rain drops, and without the bursting. Just a slow deep moderation that eventually covers my arms and back and head and redefines me as slow motion melancholy. I am down on the earth. A smell, a breeze of cool eucalyptus coming up through the cracks and there is a guttural hymn deep and stoic and sincere.

"Stand by me
Stand by me
Lord you never lost a battle
Stand by me"

Laying on my side I make a pillow of an arm crook and wander off to the depth of the sky

He's no longer dreaming, not sleeping, but he keeps his eyes closed and rolls over to the cold part of the pillow, waiting for the song to drift back up. It's morning in the west. The sun pushing out trailing pools of nocturne, painting a replacement in warm earth tones. The wind dips and picks up speed down the mountain side, heating the backs and faces of wandering raconteurs, those who are up and out at such an early hour.

Not yet unpacked, half crushed boxes fill the room, leaning against each other and walls at dangerous angles. Sitting on the edge of the bed, cracking his knuckles, neck, yawning and stretching tense muscles till they seem about to pop. Walking barefoot across the transition of carpet to cheap faded linoleum, feeling feet stick and peel, the yellow pallor film with the swooping blue designs looking more like the flayed, tattooed skin of a drunken sailor, than kitchen flooring. Grab a tecate from the counter before moving to the only chair in the room; a teal-blue plush rocking number that'd been found on a street corner or inherited from a neighbor several apt's ago.

Crouched, feet on the chair, taking large gulps from the room temperature beer and rocking in slow rhythm to the sound of the Hollywood freeway to the north or east. Opening a box marked CLOTHES, scrawled in the capital black letters of someone else's handwriting-

Contents: 1. half pint of Black Velvet
2. bag of weed
3. grip of records:
a. Jimmy Rogers - Chicago Bound
b. Aretha Franklin - Young, Gifted & Black
c. The Gun Club - Pastoral Hide & Seek
d. Waits - The Early Years
e. King Sunny Ade - Best of the Classic Years
f. Sonny Rollins w/ the Modern Jazz Quartet
g. Sleater Kinney - Sleater Kinney
piled on top of   4. pots and pans.

Inspection reveals no clothes. Dropping the needle on Waits, dragging hands through each pocket and pouch of his backpack for some zig-zags, Tom praying coarsely about dodging the pitfalls of love.

Sitting now, properly, same chair, he lights a camel, catching the first peppery draw of tobacco on his tongue. Breaking up the weed on the back of the record sleeve out of deference to Toms young face. Sparking the j, quick pull of whisky, exhale. Salivary glands ride the mix of bitter sweet whiskey weed smoke, pushing away from the dock for a slow summer boat ride in the park type day. Catching the crisp river of breeze gently wheezing at his edges and, realizing he isn't dressed, pulling on an undershirt and a pair of brown slacks, try to smooth the wrinkles with his palms, flip the record and back to crouching in the chair, lighting cigarettes and taking drags of whiskey as he sees fit the day to dictate.

After an hour or so, after the initial high has wandered off and the inward philosophical assault has mellowed, he begins to see the city again. His rooms at the Dicksboro with their views of Vermont Ave and eastward, north past Hollywood Blvd with it's stars no one who lives here talks about or cares to look at, up over the hills through Nichols Canyon or Outpost, up to the rim of the city where Mulholland snakes for miles toward the Pacific.

This, his first morning in the apartment. Crouched rocking in front of the window, the thin black woven screen with its little holes and cobwebs seems to refresh his view with a flutter at each movement. He drags the rocker to a different window to watch enthusiastically, the unflinching Downtown skyline . The clustered black buildings of all shapes and sizes, the formed pods filled with people seem to stretch and settle with the dawn, to hunker down separately to face the day.

This city resets at night. There's a shelter in the darkness, from which spring shimmering facades, the cosmic tents bursting with light, insides flowing out to the streets, bolstering courage and beckoning with hedonist promises. But then, he hasn't been here long enough to know what the city does at night. Spent time in LA over the years. Visiting friends, for days on end sometimes. Denting couches with worn out corpse. But this is new daily terrain, new days and nights of sweaty flesh he'll have to learn the patterns of. Learn to caress and ignore and forget and rediscover.

Hit the lobby, the street, the screen door of the mercado with his nose as he tries to push through a pull only. Not the most desirable introduction to the neighborhood grocer but he laughs it off and the squat woman behind the counter hasn't seemed to notice. Grab a basket, picking through the produce, swatting away a few tenacious fly's, looking for stuff that is furthest from spoiling. This is one of those places where the avocados are 25cents a piece but you gotta work for it. Filling the basket with cans, fruits, vegetables, moving to the meat counter in back that looks like it might be not quite cold enough and ordering a pound of chicken, surveying the seafood for a later date. He walks out with $50 worth of Ralph's or Trader Joes for a cool fifteen. This is his kind of place. A joint for discerning tastes and wallets.

In the kitchen he makes breakfast with the pans from the box marked clothes. Eggs, jalapeños, beans and tortillas. He dices tomatillos, showering them over top with a scoop of queso fresco. Putting on the Sonny Rollins/Modern Jazz lp, walking the room, eating, thinking seriously on the interior situation. Having set up only his bed and record player the day prior, he tries to picture the room and his belongings and how they will occupy this space.

By noon he has unpacked most of the boxes, which, folding and shoving with necessary violence, he stores in the back of the closet. He can stand in the middle of the room with everything spread around him to the white walls, little paths careening through the apartment. The ceiling fan clicks it's accompaniment. Shuffling and stacking the books into the bookcase he'd built, into the existing shelves with the little glass windows built off the kitchen counters.

He takes a beer and wanders past the neighbors doors to the open fire escape window. Stepping through, imitation of a sweaty crab. Looking down through the black steel frame, at the bolts that keep him tethered to the building, how old they are. Feeling like waiting to fall.

A middle aged woman with wild hair washes her car in the still afternoon. Watching her to take his mind off the concrete below. The bums squat against the wall at Saver Liquor, or sprawl across a small staircase under the windows, going in and out, smoking cigarettes, asking people on the way to the laundromat, on the way from the barbershop, for spare change.

Finishing the beer and stepping from his suspension back-in-of-doors, past the old elevator with its gold accordion grate, to his room and the continued move and stack, hang and ponder, opening, closing of drawers and cabinets, hammer and nail and stand at the window watching the passers by who compose routines that move the city to dance.

Around four he has nearly finished. Finished the whiskey, finished the cigarettes, the weed and most of the unpacking. Doing his wobbly best to stack file hang and suspend the whole of his life and possessions into their little compartments. Floating on nostalgia, oblivious to the current motion of arms and legs, through all the rooms he's packed and unpacked over the years. All the couches in their corners or mattresses on the floor with rumpled covers that would have looked uncomfortable pulled and folded slick and taught. Wondering what where when why and how all those previous roommates are doing now.

Where is Mark? Middle aged and liquor selling back then, with his high on the hill house, its 300 degree views of the ocean where he'd rented a room. The 24/7 above ground jacuzzi bubbling and whirring on the wooden deck beneath the pepper tree, dripping constant in the chlorine steam. With the stained glass bar lamps glowing above the pool table. Mark who never left the garage to use any of these things, where he smoked his cigarillos, drank his bourbon and watched the speed channel or Hollywood action blockbusters till 4 am. His custom 54 chevy, its intake chrome pipes jutting up through the hood, stoically waiting for the next car show to strut and gleam in the sun. Paul's room, white walls lined with books waist high and the cabinet/table he'd built, covered with candles secured to the top in their melting, birthplace to the jagged scrawlings of his fractured pencil thoughts. Where he'd bought his first mattress (all the others hand-me-downs), ignorant to sizing, he'd gone with cheap. Unpacking it from the box (the dimensions of which should have been a clue) and laying it on the floor, it looked small. Like, child small. A girl he brought home laughed and told him it was a crib mattress. Asked if his Mickey Mouse sheets were in the wash. Legs dangling off the end at the calves as he dreamed long forgotten scenes at night.

Pete Lymon's Motor Lodge at seventeen, with the speed,

schwag, broken t.v., plastic cups and sinks for ashtrays, hot plate, maid service, living out of a backpack with revolving faces crashed out, plastered to the cheap carpet for days and weeks.

His first apartment, the two level condo he'd shared with Andre when they were 18. Picture of a young Madonna above the downstairs toilet, topless with great (80's) tits, cigarette sexually semi-hard on her lip. A hole in the wall at the bottom of the staircase where he'd put his fist trying to stop the forward motion of riding a beer box down the carpeted stairs (first experience with deposits, and not getting them back). The balcony with it's 60' drop where, after parties, the guests who hadn't made it home would sit or stand, maneuvering a cheap collapsible fishing pole, trying to retrieve the nights debris of broken chairs or boxes from the sidewalk bellow. Where Monica's pet chinchilla - let loose the night before by Jerry the drunk tweaker from next door - would hide behind the upright piano and scramble across the keys at twilight and daybreak. On Sundays they'd make a run to the recycling center, Paul's blue van loaded with broken leaking body bags of bottles and cans, the weeks dead soldiers collected and co-opted for 60 or 70 bucks. Exchanged for more beer on the way home. Nights, Andre would come home from his security job to find them stacking empty cans into pillars on the perma-sticky glass coffee table, the seventeenth can wedged in at the ceiling. The game had developed organically toward a goal of seeing how many of these pillars could be erected before the whole thing came toppling down in a nearly empty clanging rain of aluminum and backwash hops.

There was the apartment off Via Angelina with no electricity the first two weeks. Where he'd run an extension cord out the front door and down the winding staircase to the hallway outlet, borrowing enough energy to run a lamp and a little stereo. One evening the light flickered and extinguished, the stereo green/blue glow and the music dissolved in darkness. Following the orange cord to the wall plug he found it severed, cleanly cut by some neighbor with a pair of scissors, either unafraid or unaware of what Paul saw as the danger of using something sharp and metal to cut a live wire.

This, the dicksboro is his first pad solo. Seated high in the sky, corner of the building. where he can look down at Oaxaca Market with its blue brick and painted signs. With its mural of a different

Madonna, two dimensional knockoff of a Diego Rivera with red and gold beams of righteous piety radiating north east west. He has taped pictures of Iggy, James Brown and Howllin' Wolf, prints of paintings by Sylvia Ji and Harvey Dinnerstein above the stove. All to develop a film of grease in the weeks and months to come. In a built-in dresser drawer, he finds a message written in black sharpie.

lived here oct.1 '94 - oct. 1 '95 Mad cockroaches but had a great time

Paul has never cared for cockroaches, but is always searching for a good time.

A thin middle aged woman in an empty house, defined by an attractive melancholy, is standing in a sparsely decorated hacienda style living room. She's noticed what looks like a hole in the bottom of the wall where it meets the floor. I notice her notice it. She cannot see me. I am her, but she is not me. Walking over to said wall, she carefully bends over onto one knee, only then seeing that there is a whole section of the wall missing. She lays down prone on her belly. Looking into a room she's never seen connected to the house she has lived in for nearly 15 years. It looks like a butchering room, with oversized orange floor tiles, dirty grout and a draining grate. Straining to get her head through the narrow space in the wall she realizes it has opened to a doorway and she's now laying unnecessarily in the threshold to the room. Standing and walking in, she feels the air as electrical distortion in her cells. Zap zap Zap and she is in a valley with high snowcapped mountains to her right and a brooding swamp-like forest to the left. the rain starts and the days and nights seem to fly by in fast forward. Standing in a combined state of petrification and awe when suddenly, from a distant hilltop, tiny flares erupt from what appears to be a mountainside cave. A bullet whips past and she realizes someone is shooting at her. More points of light appear from more gunmen. She flies into the forest and as soon as she passes the preliminary line of trees she looks back over her shoulder, seeing only dark trunks and limbs bearded with moss. Slowing her steps and returning her gaze forward she tries to stop from running into a brick wall which shatters on impact, finding herself standing, once again in her familiar hacienda style living room.

Unable to tell the time based on the light outside. Either early morning before sunrise, or sometime past sunset, one day or the other. He will stop drinking tomorrow (today?), he resolves. It's most likely Wednesday or Thursday. Which one specifically? Who can say. Regardless, his schedule has been clear for some time now. He needs water but a hand finds a bottle unconsciously, lips tugging burning liquid nipple, calm warm settling. Inhale. Exhale. Burn. Shuttering chapped eyes with burning lids. Return to sleep.

Sitting, eating pizza at a white table he can see through a spot in the torn corner of a red table cloth. Pepperoni with jalapeños, blotting hot sauce on every other bite. Something catches in his throat and the body goes numb in frozen terror. This is choking. With one hand cupping the other fist he jams into the solar plexus in some learned from a movie personal Heimlich. In this moment, all air still completely blocked, inside the feeling of a capped collapsed bottle, void of air. He can remember his mother telling him in one of her fear of him living alone tips— to ram himself into the corner of a table, corner of a couch. This seems crazy, even now.

He is breathing again. A chunk of wet pizza soaking atop the half eaten slice. He is thinking that there is a person who is not him that would go for round two on that piece. Wrapping it in a napkin and setting it aside before taking a long drink of root beer. Inhale four seconds, hold seven seconds, exhale twelve seconds. This is something else his mother has told him. A breathing exercise to calm himself. Ease the tension she knows he is constantly building inside.

The reflection in the window to his left seems not to recognize what has almost just happened. A top 40 station plays radio pop and a doughy voiced DJ announces the latest Disney tween robot who's made the move from bright eyed sassy to cat eye fuck me. Until the day when people turn malicious on their creation, relegating her to the front pages of register rack tabloids and stays in hospitals for 'exhaustion'. Feeding new meat into the grinder, a perpetual motion machine of parasitic creation.

He feels guilty. A hard to pinpoint feeling, like guilt. It's a foreboding maybe, that strikes him occasionally when he realizes that everything and everyone is for sale and the price is everything or nothing, depending on which side you listen to. Noises of clang and bash, Spanish, the ring of the telephone wafting on wings of garlic. They make subs here too, and calzones, which as near as Paul can tell, are pizza burritos. Maybe burritos are Mexican calzones. He will find out later which came first. Or not.

Standing out front, the cooling night air laps at his face and ears and he's glad to have worn a sweater. Lighting a cigarette, warmth of the smoke as the filter crushes slightly between his fingers. Walking now.

With gleaming teeth and swollen yellow prostates I see them. In mausoleums and fall out shelters where the women bake stews and break their backs baptizing chickens in wholly water. Sitting with tongues tied to lampposts and cigarettes. All the while unintelligible banshee whales ooze from the lips of the children, the dying and the insane. Hearts made of stolen vegetables lower cranes dangling mind maze fortitude freewheeling delights. Trains with crocodile eyes. Lighting quick darkness. The men stand in corners, passed out from waiting around on bus benches, against telephone poles belching radiator fog nocturne. A whistle blows in the distance. Two long bright bursts of shade jump out to form shadows. Window shattering wind. Mostly no one pays me any mind.

Waking in the tungsten glow of electric night, slumped against the dumpster behind a grocery store. Righting himself, shakily, he begins the long stumble home. Finding a bottle in some buried deep for secrets jacket pocket he drinks deeply. Stopping to steady himself against the alley wall where he pounds the rest of the bottle, feeling the burning. Loving the burning. The body aches. Breathing labored, take a hit from the inhaler that luckily has remained in his pocket.

Now again he wakes. Slowly, comfortably, opening his eyes on a strange bed, suddenly full of foreboding. The smell of unfamiliar linens and regret. Looking around. Getting up, he's fully clothed and, finding his converse kicked off in a corner, he slips his feet in, flattening the heels, and wanders out into a room filled with maps and gadgets and copper instruments, magnifying lamps and tables and books and files. It's a well lit room owing mostly to a large round window, below which floats a head, blanket covered, tussock of brown hair peeking from beneath couch sleeping.

Excuse me. Where am I? He asks. The blanket sliding down to reveal a young woman's face. This is Greg's house man.

How'd I get here?

You just walked in through the front door last night. She props herself up on an elbow and yawns. You just walked in and laid down in that bed and passed out. He follows her eyes to the room and the bed with the smell that isn't his but lingers on him.

Where's Greg?

Greg's at work.

What does he do?

He's an architect.

This would account for the decor, he decides.

I really appreciate you letting me crash here.

Yeah, greg tripped out a little when he got home and saw you in his bed, but he's a pretty mellow dude.

Tell him thanks.

Outside, looking hard at the door for a full minute, waiting for some remembrance of stopping here, last night. Searching for some familiarity. Does any part of this scene seem evocative of a place he knows. In his drunkenness could he have mistaken this for friendly territory? But there is nothing. No similarities.

Walking around a while to get his bearings, he doesn't, and so drops on a nearby bus bench sweating whiskey bullets as he sits. Lucky it's a stop with a bench. His phone is dead and there's really no one to call. There's a chance this bus runs somewhere that's home or near it. With enough change in his pockets for one transfer, hoping it's enough. Waiting. The streets are dead, and being alone at a stop can mean you've got a while to wait. Finally the orange cartoon face of a bus, the scrolling LED panel, the air brakes that stab at the curb. Boarding, the driver tells him the fare machine's busted. He'll get at least one free ride today.

Lumbering down the tree lined streets, bouncing over each pothole, feeling like connected to the dilapidated roads of Los Angeles. Feeling dilapidated. It starts to rain. Large drops fall, the windshield plowing forward. This aluminum ecosystem with its ever-changing biotic and abiotic components forging ahead. He's not quite far away enough yet from the blackout. Not far enough to feel the fear, regret, remorse, he knows are coming, are here already, but they will build with their lingering. So staring out the window, leaning forehead to plexiglass, he tries to think of things that are cold, and not throbbing.

Feeling his own heart beating. Seeing it in the short jumping of his stomach. He does not like this. The sensation of the mechanisms of his body. He should like it. These signs, subtle, prove he is alive. That blue blood (he'd heard that once, that blood was blue inside the body. Never bothered to check. Thats why veins are blue, right? Everything seems probable) pumps through him, lubricating nourishing restoring, all the highways and byways of his fleshy body sack.

For this same reason, he's put off by the inflating band of the blood pressure cuff. Its purring choke around his bicep. Ballooning around him, heartbeat becoming centralized in the arm, as if it had lived there all along. A closing in feeling, pulse escalating, sure to stop at any second, explode in silence. Then the numbers he never understands. Something over something. Is that bad?

It's a little high, but nothing serious. Do you exercise?

No.

It must be fine, he'd think. Factoring in the anxiety at the rim of these near panic attacks would probably lower the numbers to sustainable levels.

He's been in the little anteroom of the apartment for hours. Smoking cigarettes. Painting the face of a woman on top of the torso. So intent and single minded he'd missed the sun's going, the waining light transitioning to dark and the coiling chain of cigarettes he's piled. Pleased with his progress, pushing up to his feet & stepping back. The head is too big. Looks absurd. A bobble head, top heavy on a toy body. Shit. He should have checked from different perspectives.

Wandering out to the dim shadows of the main room. Fish tank window glow of neon pale blue on the walls. Clicking ceiling fan spin. Knowing the fruit flys asleep, sucking dreams and grease in the glazed slick kitchen, above the trashcan, next to the damaged pictures on the walls, curling at the edges.

He sits listening for the sound of trains, rumbling and sweeping through the tunnels 6 floors below him. At his folks place, in the dead hours of those stubborn suburban seaside nights, he'd listen to the whoop of freights steadily crawling through the San Juan Capistrano depot. On winter mornings, before dawn, the fishermen still stowing gear and speaking softly over the rims of coffee cups, white styrofoam half melting with heat. The foghorn echo off the sandy cliff faces. Searching through the mist. Over the steady salt water's churn, up the hill through the intersection at PCH. Up still & always moving, past the Latin Quarter, the small apartments where chickens slept, out in the yards, their oiled feathers distilling the fog into dew. And, after touching all of these things, up into the ears of a boy on the 2nd floor, who knew the world was full of clippers and submersibles and spacecraft, cowboys & bluesmen, a place called Funafuti & everything. If he could just reach out to touch them. To be sure they were real.

After smoking a bowl & pouring three fingers of bourbon into a coffee cup, he lets the door shut its mechanical arm behind. Sip the bourbon, the golden elevator gliding to a shudder. Into the lobby. Out the side door… No, first down three, then up two stairs. Out the side door. Through the small parking lot reserved for tenants. Across Berendo. Sip the bourbon in the faux racing seat and play Cruisin' USA at the choice-of-two laundromat arcade.

He hasn't said a word in three days. Up on the sixth floor. Out on buses. Underground on trains. Hasn't worked for some months. Only lately noticing the money drying up. That is the liquid nature of dough. Especially with nothing added to the pot. But that'd been the plan. He'd lived with his folks for a year to save the bread. Cash in the bank to boil & steam away the toxic nodules that had accumulated since his last real vacation. So he'd moved to the Dicksboro. K-Town, Los Angeles 90049. USA. Paul wanted nothing to distract him. No work, no woman. Full penetration of the streets. Days of foreplay. Fragrant carnal nights with all the demons and angels who move like streams, feed on hustle.

But he lost track of himself at some point. Like he always does. 3 days ago he bought a case of beer, glass 1/5th of admiral Nelson rum & a plastic gallon of Barton's. A silence had to be achieved. Some kind of equilibrium. Paul wanted silent commune with the nature designed built fortified, by that group of humanity that sees an empty space & tries to fill it in all three dimensions. Assaulting, exploiting the senses. A nature of a different nature.

So for three days & 3 nights he hasn't spoken. Thinks it's three days. At some point he'd unburdened himself of time. Days or nights popping in and out around him, without any practical use or definition. He read, even remembered some of it. Watched the shadows creep & recede on the street below. Created stories of lives for the waiting/scurrying lines of people arriving and departing the Vermont/Beverly subway station. He lay in bed, on the floor, in the bath. Lukewarm water ejaculating intermittently from the shower head. Ate some of those strawberries that go bad the instant you decide to buy them. He walked Vermont to the arcade with a rum & coke, feeding quarters into the machines. Watching a guy play the most cardiovascular game of Dance Dance Revolution, feeling his own chest begin to clench. He walked around La Luz de Jesus, Skylight Books. Got all the way west to the Santa Monica Pier, watching the squat latinos, the wiry asians, chopping bait, cast clear smooth filament into shimmering pools of sunset glitter and froth. Pressing his weight against the strong support beams of the Ferris Wheel, picture the legs of a prone juggler manipulating geometrically obtuse objects, rolling barrels on snug fabric slippers.

He found a book on Gordon Parks. Feeling bad but sticking with the plan, bought it without a word to the woman behind the counter. Shaded up against the pylons in the sand, he takes a beer from the backpack and tries to digest Parks' images. Everything vulnerable, everything contrast. Each expressing some calm deep truth in a moment.

When he looks back up to the sun soaked beach, every light color disappears into the sky like unpainted gaps in time, exposed canvas. Feeling the whole scene shift into timelessness. No different than it has always been, will always be.

The great dark collapse. The churning hollow gorge of the sea, deep and brilliant— full of the improbable, the unlike, the glowing eyeless masses being worked at in all directions by atmospheres of pressure and sleepless eroding forces. Salt wind and what must be the particles of millennia of decomposing flesh, shell, ebb, flotsam and beach foam nipping at the pipers scurry.

Paul is petrified by the enormity of it. Caverns and creatures man will never, could never see. Places and things you would wish unseeing when they trap you at night in your dreams dark and strangling. It is intriguing, the sea. He is calmed by the sound of the waves and the ceaselessness. Liking it most standing near, on the pummeled sand alone. On days when the sky seems to strain out of the dark blue green, whitecaps and rock boils and quiet calm reefs going about their business. The heavens meeting the Pacific in the woven edge of a Mexican blanket. Birds of all shapes and sizes dotting the cliffs and the water, floating like voices down a hall. Wondering how far this frequency will carry them. Distance. Heavy and sad and comfortable and wanting.

On the pier Paul wonders if someone can share in this quiet and it seems true. True in a thousand different ways and faces. And each feeling is amplified by that second person and the comfort is almost like a consuming fire and the aloneness is nearly unbearable and every wave is sad and full and forever. He is content for now and, putting the cigarette butt in his pocket, heads back toward the road. Watching the planks like a conveyor belt disappear beneath him.

Inadvertently he steps into the public pulpit of a tall & animated philosopher. His finger and arm, his every convulsion slashing the air. Battering the small congregation and passers-by with machine gun fire questions;

What systems do we have in place to hear from the homeless, the addicted, the disenfranchised? Where in the democratic process can these voices be heard first hand, rather than from the talking heads of spokespeople with no experience themselves? How can we, the people, even stay in step with the politics & policies & agendas of each side and group and lobby in a 24 hour capitalist partisan news cycle? How can we choose leaders we know will break promises, running on vague campaign slogans that rely on the psychological appeals of advertising and repetition rather than truth of information? What can we do about an incestuous government culture that is bought and sold & redistricted, with policies worded like the misdirect of a magic trick? How do we deal with the global corporate appropriation of slavery, bigger than ever & without borders of color or continent, religion or sexual preference? This new caste system with ever dwindling rungs & ever increasing gaps, set at such as steep angle as to make upward mobility most difficult. What do we do when political ideas and party affiliations are passed down through generations without thought to personal relevancy or a changing social, cultural & economic landscape....

At his feet is a small box, neatly labeled:
Citizenry for the Protec-
tion of Equality & Reform
in Democracy

15 minutes later, Paul sits at the bus station, the tall philosopher & his box of donations heading towards him. He can smell the
joint before he sees it. Pretty good speech back there, to the sweaty
preacher who settles on the bench. Thanks. Seemingly having lost
his earlier verbosity. Paul watches the man, wondering about him.
Wanting, like this man, to be striking out for a cause, a crusader for
the downhearted, to have that fervor of community, the steeliness of
fighting for the greater good. Head buzzing. Feeling from the beer
like floating. The preacher flicking the roach. Looking tense. Head
shaking before he bursts out:

Lay off me man. It's nothing. It's about nothing but what's
in this little box right here. The coins and bills scratching the walls of
his collection cube. It's about $ & getting what you need to survive.
It's about giving people a scapegoat for their shitty lives and getting
some money to pay for my daughters diabetes meds. He is calm,
defeated, tired eyes almost shut. Have you ever read Elmer Gantry,
Paul asks. No man. Fuck Elmer Gantry.

Watching the tall philosopher round the corner, he understands. The man is right. It is about doing what you have to do. He
feels this stranger. Feels bad. Whether his daughter is sick, whether
there even is a daughter doesn't matter. Here is a man doing what
he has to do. No one would be out here, swinging for the fences like
that if they didn't feel they had to be. Most people don't even get a
chance to choose, we find ourselves, surrounded by lives we don't remember making, bound to decisions we never knew were important.
He wants to catch up to him. Tell him it's all some beautiful dream.
But he can't. And he doesn't know if he believes it himself.

A white spider made of dust tumbles through the desert on quick winds clutching after its web, legs touching down now and then to stumble, set on its course, tiny heart beating exhaustedly, flailing in panic and illusory luck.

Gagging. Running to the bathroom to barely make most of the bright yellow/green bile into the sink. Sitting down on the toilet to breath a moment. Wet some toilet paper and clean the thick slime where he's missed the mark. Brushing his teeth gently, gingerly, to avoid more gut wrenching. Watching a brown silverfish with yellow stripes at the joints, and five long yellow antennae, wandering around the sink bowl. Trying one angle and the next to climb up its porcelain prison walls, only to fail and stop for recollection of purpose. Feeling around for food most likely. What do they eat? do they eat? Or do they just get stuck in sink bowls and die? On cutting boards and in showers. Not a luxurious diet he reasons. They could eat dirt and skin and rot outside, why come in here to almost certain death? How little they must understand. Do they die when you send 'em packing down the drain pipes? They must have lungs, or not. Do all multicellular creatures have lungs or gills? What about photosynthesis. Could these prehistoric looking fools, descended perhaps from trilobites, get their breath through the absorptions of those antenna. Paul bids him farewell before engaging the water, watching it baptize his adventurer for a few seconds before rerouting it down the drain.

He's been shitting black liquid & puking bile for weeks. Needing change but putting it off 'till tomorrow. Unable to eat, or even drink tea, till he's had a few drinks to calm his stomach. He assumes the black stool means blood. Probably his stomach lining, tired and disheartened. So he resolved to find an AA meeting. All the ones he sees online around him are Spanish speaking. He'd like to get away for the day, just the right distance from home, to Venice. Feels he'll need to remove himself from his regular surroundings to make it through the hour. It's not his first rodeo with a twelve step program, with AA. He's been in and out over the years. Never got much time, maybe a week. Never had a sponsor or did the steps. Removing to the streets without a drink. Maybe this time will be different.

In the dim yellow room, small, storage closet-esq, jammed with circles of chairs, filled with sober people glad handing, seeming to have known each other intimately for years, Paul finds a hard metal seat without a pair of keys or a business card denoting reserved and sips the coffee provided. 10 min in he's appalled by the bitching. Tries to stick it out. A woman breaks down in tears about her life.

The state of her personal and family affairs. She has a gold watch the size of a fist, jeweled with stones so big they shine even under these shitty depressing lights. She says she's lost everything, but this watch tells a different story. Maybe it's fake then. Maybe so. But, if all is lost, why cling to these ghosts of opulence? Should this not have been a lesson to her about the coveting of objects, about the illusion, the ephemeral nature of monetary success? Several more people break down, the room waiting in silence for them to compose and continue.

Paul half listens to some guy rap at him while they finish coffee and cigarettes after the meeting in the parking lot. This stranger, greasy and loud, wanting to tell all about how much better off he is in sobriety, wife... job.... kids... He wears a blue tennis shirt thats too big, tucked unsystematically into tight high waters ornamented, like the star atop a christmas tree, with a flaking gold buckle holding together a cracked woven leather belt. Paul thanks him and shakes his wet hand. Rounding the corner he wipes the mans transferred grease off on his bandana holstering it back into his pocket.

Finding a nearby patch of sand, he sits and lights a cigarette. A boy walks along the waters edge amongst the larger rocks that slowly crawl away from the base of the cliffs. The tide must have been high, surging froth and erosion earlier, but it has subsided, leaving a residue of slick oily blackness creeping down the sides of rocks, pooling in their crevices. The boy is young. Paul is a poor judge of age but he cant be older than seven, his younger brother following more awkwardly behind him. They are fair and blond, identically dressed in denim shorts and white t-shirts. Paul tries not to think of the Hitler youth but fails. The older child, looking around for his mother, shouts suddenly.

I'm trapped. The path is very slippery on both sides. I don't know what to do.

Paul finds himself moved nearly to tears by the insight. Wanting to shout back at the kid that that feeling never goes away.
On the way home he stops to buy a jug of wine and a precooked chicken. They must have put it under the heat lamp just before he got there so, even by the time he gets home and rips open the plasticy paper of the bag, it's still moist rosemary greasy and, cutting pieces off or pulling at the legs, he sits in his room pouring the Carlo Rossi

Paisano wine and eating the chicken, elbows on the edge of a shiny smooth-from-use flea market dinner tray with the aluminum rim.

When he buys jug wine he always buys Carlo Rossi, and when he buys Carlo Rossi he always buys Paisano. It's like mainlining the aura of Tortilla Flats. That was a town Paul could have done well in. Or felt like he was doing well in. Everybody just went day to day trying to scrape up the dough for a 15¢ jug of wine to share amongst whoever put in, and whoever didn't. There were a few scoundrels but they all seemed to have good intentions at heart.

Lower the needle on a record of works by Jean Philippe Rameu, a cat who wrote and played harpsichord tunes back in the mid 16th century. According to the record sleeve Jean really turned Paris on its ear. Trying not to get grease or wine on the dirty record sleeve, Paul reads a nearly incomprehensible academic study on the place of keyboard in french high society of the day. Things like "... in a common key and many of them in the simple rondo form, abaca, with an easily remembered principal refrain alternating with two interludes or reprises." and "As for Rameau himself, his interest was in building new music for his own day, not a hypothetical music of the future. It took a Richard Wagner to coin that unfortunate term..."

He tries picturing himself in old Jean's time, sleeves rolled up holding his jug of wine, in the middle of a gaudy gold and green ballroom lit by dripping candles with girdle waisted buxom women sashaying or preening and top hatted garish men drinking and standing near white columned walls, the fatter ones sitting at tables sipping from small glasses, sucking their lips and chortling.

He's wondering how they lit chandeliers back in the day. Not ladders. They only had the straight ladders you had to lean against something. He isn't sure but that seems right. They must have been lowered down with chains, lit the candles and raised them back up, cleating them to the wall. Those who owned chandeliers, the rich, wouldn't have lit them themselves, wouldn't have thought to. Probably still cant and don't.

Walking out of Saver Liquor. Slap. The pack of Camel Filters against his palm. 4x. Spin. Repeat. Notice the local homeless, painted against the blue sided wall. Theirs are jerking, shrinking, expanding shadows that speak soft (for the moment) and slow. Moods transitioning with the dusk. Crack the plastic restraints and take a quick sip of flourishing joy from the new whiskey bottle, turning back into the green wash of the store. The light, the feel of it on his skin he would describe as fluoride. It's good, swimming through the fluoride. Buy the shadows a case of Tecate and take it out to them.

Their spokesman Antonio. Short. A sort of swollen jetting jaw line, gristle stubble writhing in the headlights that beat quick across his face. Thank you my friend, Antonio says, offering a hand Paul can see is cloistered in several layers of gunk. Hey, no problem. They're all yours. Shaking the hand before, discreetly, trying to wipe it on the back of his pants without offending his new companions. The other 3, taking beers, popping the tops, each offering a hand, a subdued, gracias amigo, gracias a usted, thank you. Then the slow sucking sound of the first sip of beer from a can. A proffered cheers from Antonio. Gulp from the bottle.

Five men sitting against the wall, silhouettes. Them drinking the beer, he the Jim Beam. Antonio acting as interpreter for a conversation which started tentative and clunky, but has quickly grown more relaxed. Paul offering up as much Spanish as he can. They tell stories, constant punctuations and interjections adding to the scenes being memorialized. Corrections. Nods of agreement.

He feels warm, feels like a million broken pieces, feels the flesh pinching between his tailbone and the concrete, his spine and the wall, helping him decide they would be more comfortable in the apartment, out from under the potential scrutiny of passers by or cops, so he invites them up. "Vamanos a mi apartmento con el cerveza." he offers the group. Never sure if his Spanish is looked at as pandering. Knowing it is, also, not great.

He is often concerned, as a straight white man, that he is ignorant of how to act around different cultures, minorities (& majorities for that matter) and women. He is worried that there may be indoctrinated bullshit in his mind he is not even aware of. He knows there is, and tries to search out and eradicate these bullshits.

Being uneasy with people, he places himself under the magnifying glass of books, music, film; Art! The art of the disenfranchised. Art with an axe to grind. And it's not always easy to find this non-white or non-male art. But this time it's fine. Everyone agrees this is a good plan. Stiffly, and with some confusion, they begin to stand and gather their things. Taking the empty cans to the dumpster and turning back to the group, watching the silhouettes bleeding one into the other, he feels as if they (himself included) have stepped from the background of a painting, unready for this world.

Leading the procession into his apartment, apologizing for the mess, assuming the tone and guise of a carnival barker, he throws back his head and in his deepest voice shouts at a whisper; Welcome! Bienvenidos! Watching them enter single file over his shoulder as they pass through the thin corridor leading to the main room. They must have looked a motley crew waiting vainly, sipping beer at the elevator in the empty lobby. Or marching up the staircase, bodies sloshing, lazy low mumble as they climbed the six floors to his room.

Paul is trying to figure a seating arrangement while Antonio, half muses/half asks about the way each floor has a distinct smell and color. The tallest and oldest looking of the group (Paul thinks of every weathered vaquero in every cowboy movie and wonders if this man, whose name he hadn't caught, has ever rode a horse) is now perusing his bookshelves. Leaning in from a distance, hands behind his back, long body bent at the joint, looking through the spines smiling.

Sitting them, best he can, around the room, finally able to take in their individuality, to separate their unique features. The shortest, in the plush teal chair, rocking pleasantly, seems to be made entirely without angles. Arms, eyes, hips, lips, nose, ears, all rounded by baby fat. Our tall vaquero on the bed, looking every inch a leather muppet, with another man who Paul only remembers as being graceful as fuck. Antonio, his broad, flat face framed in the oily brown strands that stick to his forehead, broken teeth stained the color of river-bank mud, sits in the middle. Well, not like an interrogation, but like, across from Paul who, picking a record, offers the cover to the group for inspection. Hoping they wont think it presumptuous or pandering (again) that he's picked Antonio Aguilar. At the very least the old man'll be on board, he thinks. As always, his fears are mis-guided and, with the drunk group soberly and almost congratulatory accepting his decision, gravity gets hold of a crackle of vinyl, taking his seat as the first honey-smooth notes roll over them. Arms raised. Salud.

Their conversation continues as before and each man gets up in turns to fetch more beer from the fridge or head to the john, or both. They compliment him on his apartment, his taste in music. All at once, the graceful one leaps into a dance as if spurred by some spirit from his future, moving elegantly around the room before falling onto the bed to the applause and whistles of all present. Between songs the silences open, new avenues of dialogue forming in each mans half consciousness, passing around a pack of camels, letting the scene breath, plugging the silence now, as a group, at the spouts of bottles and cans, steeling themselves against the precarious nature of the moment. Or maybe they are just drunks, sucking at the teat of comfort, looking to disappear.

Where do you come from Antonio? Paul asks. Ciudad de Juarez, the proud reply, showing the group a tattoo on his bicep. My mother and father still live there. I'd like to go back to visit, but how can I? He smiles into the mouth of the can and takes a long drink. Even if I could, who can say if I would. Seeming to be thinking about it for the first time, his eyes look lively for a prolonged instant.

Paul wonders if he is thinking about them now, if he is wondering about questions that have not been asked, if he is reliving things that will not/cannot be told, or if, like Paul, he has just stopped to wonder at this situation, this room with these people and the hows and whys of finding themselves here.

The old vaquero speaks to Antonio who turns to Paul as interpreter explaining; Its very important to see your family while you can, his two sons are dead from drug violence and he doesn't want to burden his daughter. He is old and alcoholic, he thinks his daughter is better without him. And her son too, his grandson, should not have to feel the burdens of a broken man.

Switching beer between hands, a free finger pointing at a picture taped to the wall. A photo by Edward S. Curtis, famed seeker and documenter of Native American life. Paul takes a book from the shelf, full of Curtis' work, raising his bottle to toast as the vaquero's tattered digits begin delicately flipping the pages. Watching him explore the images and listening to him speak, watching the body language and hearing the congruent translation… His grandmother was an Indian, Antonio explains. He can't remember what tribe anymore, but he has small pictures in his mind. Pictures of a world…

Lighting another cigarette and replacing the pack in the center of the circle, Paul watches the man. Watches him laugh. A grin peeling back to the ears, exposing a remarkably good set of teeth or a pair of well kept dentures. Paul smiles around the circle at the others as they laugh with him. He offers the book as a gift, hoping the pictures will bring the vaquero fond memories or luck, a trade or a few bucks in a pinch. Antonio conveys the message, though the old man seems to have understood and readily accepts with many gratuities.

Short stuff is still wearing his shoes, where the other guests have removed theirs. Paul realizing in a moment of clarity that it's probably good he's drunk and they're all smoking. He guesses that the brewing smell of them (himself included- the booze leaking out, creating a thick layer of high pitched smut on his skin) could be overwhelming. But in the humor of the night, a gesture of unity, he suggests that short stuff remove his kicks and relax. There is plenty of beer left and no place they need hurry off to.

Through Antonio he declines. Thanks for the offer, he says, but his foot is hurt. Paul is about to protest when the young man partially removes the left shoe, exposing a (thus far unnoticed) swollen sock seeping varied flavors of discoloration and fluid content. Perhaps seeing the look of worry on Paul's face he offers, no money, no doctor. Resignedly. Matter of factly.

The night continues along the same bent as they work toward the bottom of the case of beer, Paul looking nearer to the clear swollen glass at the bottom of the bottle. He is searching for some weed he knows he'd had earlier. Opening every drawer, moving every stack and pile and business card (where could all these business cards have come from? He does not seek them out, but finds them in pockets, drawers, backpack, wallet, continually multiplying, being discarded, replaced) till he finds and passes a joint around the room. Offering up another cheers and looking for a new record.

Wake to the quiet ticking of the ceiling fan. A siren wail that feels as if it is moving through him. Determining what he's made of. Notice the bed sheets on the floor as he shifts his body, dragging the skin across the velcroesque fibers of the mattress. Activities of the previous night begin to traipse through his mind and he throws a glance around the room. Vague recollection of offering a space on the floor to any takers. Laughing at himself when he's finished scanning for bodies. He feels bad to be relieved they are gone. Feels anxious that he may have to see them again on an almost daily basis. How will they react if he doesn't invite them up, if he's distant, doesn't offer them money, etc?

Why had he been such a drunk? And why is that always his first question upon waking? He's glad that he was able to offer some down and out brothers a few hours of respite, but this knowledge does not dull the horror he feels toward his actions. How long can he keep on like this? Was last nights fiesta anything but detrimental to all parties involved? He tries to tell himself, as he always does at times like these, to chalk another line up on the board of experience. No other way to view these things in retrospect, or the fear would settle long and heavy. Fear of the future. Fear of his decisions, motives or lack there of, fear of consequences, the nagging fear that slowly rips at his gut and crushes all other thought from his mind.

He picks the sheets up off the floor, remembering how, after everyone had left, he'd stripped them from the bed out of fear of lice or AIDS or god knows. He'd washed his hands and stumbled on to the dirty mattress just before daybreak. Feeling bad through the whole process. That he'd reacted, after their departure, as if they were surely diseased, subhuman.

Lighting a cigarette and dragging a chair to the window, he is looking into a framed portrait of the world. The world looks into a framed portrait of him. In both the subject: little lives of little people. Riding his vision out over the rooftops to the base of the Hollywood sign, over Mulholland, circling the areas along familiar bus routes and subway exits that inhale/exhale the smooth streams of pedestrians and hawkers of wares who go about their business ignorant, and maybe better for it, of his existence.

Surprisingly there are a few beers left in the fridge. Cracking one, taking a gulp, before stirring more crystalline brown instant coffee into the mug of boiling water. He realizes he doesn't own a microwave. Many people do. Since he is just noticing it though, he must not have a need for one. Letting the coffee cool, sipping the beer, wondering how to spend the day.

He should, he will, take it easy on the booze, explore the city, avoid areas around the building where he might run into Antonio and/or the boys. He doesn't feel it in him for the day. Can't deal with whatever might exist now that he's let them into his life. People who live so close, are so in need, and him wanting to aid in their need, as repentance, justification, redemption from deeds done or left un-done, some deep self loathing or searching for relevance, a need for companionship that seems increasingly hard to suppress or fill in a healthy way. He doesn't know, but it's been decided that today isn't, can't be, the day to find out.

He's taken a long shower. Shined himself up and back into the world. Breathed in the dirty warm breeze rushing through the open shower window, highupenough that birds swoop past on currents of air bound for foreign lands. Or maybe they are cyclical like Paul. Spinning in their same saga, endlessly engaged by outside forces. Without willpower, destined to orbit the familiar.

Singing along now to Strawberry Letter 23 in his best Shuggie Otis impression, pushing eggs around a skillet. Drinking the instant coffee and smoking a camel. Swaying through the apartment to Shugg's groove. Lowering himself cross legged in the rocker, at-tempting to keep the plate level as he pours a glob of salsa on top of the eggs. Listening to the framed window world enter and mix with Shuggie, touching Paul and all the things before leaving and being replaced, through the tiny screen squares of another window. Watching the different colored sounds, their spiraling and merging clouds of separate stories collecting and colliding for an instant be-fore moving on and out.

He'd decided in the shower, water steaming, cold beer run-ning down his cheeks, mingling with the water and chest hair and washing down his body, that he will head downtown. First, pick up a back pocket of whiskey for pulling swigs discreetly on the redline or as he peruses the aisles at The Last Bookstore. Looking forward to a book/record/zine finding him between breaks where he will smoke out front, a 3D shadow against the wall, watching the city people as they go about their days, the traffic of bodies, objects, animals. Little pieces of clay riding in circles, remolded as they pass out of sight, re-entering view as new nouns.

He will meet someone. It's decided. They will share a meaningful conversation. He will start the process of entrenching himself in the creative fabric of the downtown scene. Swinging out the door of the Dicksboro he collides with short stuff, who greets him with a request for change, a cigarette, a dollar.

Short stuffs english is pretty shaky, and to be honest, Paul isn't entirely sure this is the man from the previous evening. The shoes though. Memorable discolored sock leaking out the side, any suspicion that this could be a different man quickly dissolves. Handing over a cigarette he searches for a dollar, trying not to seem like he has too much money on him. He doesn't, but is still concerned the guy might feel jilted by small change. He makes an effort at pleasantries before taking his leave, intimating he has some things to take care of. Not sure whether he feels better that the reunion has been gotten out of the way, or worried that this will become a daily occurrence.

Out of the steeping sun and into the shade. Extinguishing his cigarette and, light jog down the escalator, feeling his pockets for the plastic metro card. Falling in step through the turnstiles with the queues of people laden with backpacks, garbage bags, rolling carts, boxes of individual candies for sale, cardboard signs briefcases bikes kids with skateboards bunches of flowers newspapers books electronics. Feel the gush of warm wind signaling the oncoming train, stepping to the nearest yellow ground marker and over the clogged steel threshold to find a seat. A quick sip from the bottle as the dinging bell, the closing doors, the steady wheeze of the electric engine propels them through subterranean morning.

A man of middle age, brown skin the color of shoe leather or black tea, sitting on a bench under shake wisp trees. Big three pointed leaves sway overhead, playing on gusts of roasted breeze. Hot air blowing into Los Angeles, through, from elsewhere and back, like so many of the cities occupants. Temporary. Feverish choking wind of opening the oven and looking in. A current on which to ride the smell of dust and trash funk that the buses blow up from the gutters. Staring, this man, through strobe flash white pop of steel framing the building in front of him. Take my picture? No, just making a call, a pedestrian responds.

Noticing the man's shoeless feet. His thick socks though dirty, are without holes. It's too hot out for those socks. But it's that or dirty feet. And few opportunities to shower. His feet are probably still dirty. Socks not a great insulator.

Take my picture? The man repeats to no one. Paul has moved on.

Later, 5 min maybe, down the street silent wool footprints round the corner. Take my picture? The man a specter, seemingly everywhere at once. Paul is weary of recurrence. In such cases wondering if the universe is trying to tell him something. A warning. Or worse, his own mind, inarticulately conjuring specters to communicate.

Keeping moving, slipping wet & sipping, corner to corner. Out front of an ice cream parlor, in a impromptu theater of tourists and bystanders, a man dances jaggedly on the curb. Heavy tan gardening gloves flare out at thick tan wrists. His blue tank top faded to a pleasing pastel. The gloves, whether for aesthetics or protection, seem not to fetter the gesticulation of the hands which wave at passing cars in varied routines either practiced or improvised or divined. Conjunction of a knee bend, a head bob. The hands though, doing most of the work. Looking busy, overtired, a backpack just within reach, at the ready for a location change, waiting patiently.

The crowd dies down before he notices Paul. Or he's been waiting for this moment. Without wavering from his task (perhaps it is his penance) he speaks:

When I was in college I would smoke a lot of meth. I would stay up for days at a time, driving around banging on the steering wheel, stoping here or there to smoke a puddle and freak out a bit.

On cold mornings my skin would turn purple and I would run in place to get my circulation going again. One morning I drove out into the desert with a bag and a couple of nearly burnt out glass dicks. Parking at a rest stop I started to walk up a hill. I could see them following me. The shadows. But they had been with me for some time and I sensed no immediate danger. Next I knew, I was on top of a high ass hill and the speed was gone and they had me. I stabbed at them with the pipe. I resisted but they brought me to my knees. They forced me to smear some awful smelling cosmic paste all over my pants, my bare chest and armpits, slathering my face and hair. It wasn't until the flame was too near my nose that I realized I was alone with a half dozen empty Sterno cans and my right arm was on fire. Rolling around, screaming in the dirt. I was finally able to put it out and took off my pants and wrapped them around my arm. I collapsed. I cried. I slept half a day on that hillside. I walked back down to my car wearing boxers and boots, my pants warped around my greasy bubbling arm. That was 15 years ago today…

The next moment he's vanished. Sucked back into the ethos or the mind or an invisible gypsy caravan curating a museum of jumpers, writhers and sharps running cross country at light speeds, picking up all those whose talents are needed and deserving of preservation. Paul had only looked away for a second, the loud airhorn of a semi truck surprising his eardrums, and the man was gone. Drag the last of the bottle, setting it glinting empty atop a trashcan.

Pit stop for tacos at a truck. Queuing behind a few construction workers, boisterous in their horseplay, smiles & banter. Semi-flitartious with the older woman taking orders & collecting cash. He orders carnitas tacos and a coke, looking out for a shaded spot to enjoy a greasy lunch. Pinching the paper plate with one hand, coke sweating cold in the other, he inspects a tree for streams of ants, spiders, anything that might get creepy crawly on him if he leans against the trunk. Satisfied, against the tree now, one last look around for bugs. Cars push by, horns popping, a jackhammer from the construction site throws shards of debris from a cloud of dust. Eating the tacos. Watching women shake past. Watching the construction workers watch them.

Listening to the cat calls, it is hard for him to understand their purpose. It seems sleazy, but he's sure they're not bothered by that.

In fact, it's probably a part of the intent. The thing that confuses him is whether or not there has ever been an instance, a fuck, a date, even a smile, born from the seed of such tactics. He's never seen it do. Especially on the job. But, he supposes, it's probably more a display of masculinity; a showcasing of virility, of how meaningless and transient women are to you, rather than any practical attempt at romance. Or maybe they're just bored at work. Looking for kicks and a way to amuse each other. He doesn't know, which only serves to highlight for him how different we all really are.

Disposing of his trash and crossing the street, he wonders if they saw him. If they'd judged or speculated about him the way he had them. Maybe it's just that his mind has wandered and is hinting that he do the same. Take a pull to achieve the silence. The jackhammer stutters it monosyllabic song as he turns a corner toward quieter concrete.

Moving into the kitchen he's not entirely sure that his dream about stealing a car wasn't real. Well, if it was a dream, it wasn't real. He just can't be sure it was a dream. It seems unlikely, out of character, but daily blackouts are tough this way. When everything exists as patches of cloudy memory, pulsing fragments of things he might find out later to be true, scenes recollected with sudden pain, painted in question marks and hazy edges. Adding to the confusion a history of somewhat outlandish behavior and circumstance, enlivened by liquor, only serves to muddle the picture further, leading to believing that anything is feasible. Each time it's merely a matter of whether or not, this time, it was real. Reality usually being determined by fallout.

It's an overcast morning and he can smell the clouds drifting wetly through the apartment. He is nearly certain he had not stolen a cutlass, owing mainly to the fact that; remembering unexpectedly, Billy Crystal had been riding shotgun. But rum dreams are vivid and convincing even with their inconsistencies, and they often turn out, for Paul, to have some foot in reality. And it seems like Billy hasn't been working much in recent years….

He often dreams of flight, but only after running very fast and jumping. Most times his attempts fail. When he succeeds he can throttle around a world he has never seen, maybe never existed, touching down occasionally at a run to jump again and fly. The light in these dreams is always diffused, as if through the leaves of warm trees in dry wind. Somewhere in the Southwest or perhaps Jerusalem. There are never any cities in his sky, no people like little ants in cars or on sidewalks or clambering building up to the blue arcing line of the atmosphere trying to create noise in the vacuum of space. When he can't fly, he might be lost trying for hours days immense blocks of stand still sunlight. But his legs are heavy and refuse to run fast enough to create the lift he requires. Massage his calves and thighs to no avail. His achilles tendon like a bike chain defunct its sprocket.

When he has such dreams, he wonders what deep psychological problems might be brewing for a person to concoct such lucid failure. He knows this is one of the common ones. Like teeth falling out or a back to school scenario. He's had the teeth one too, but he thinks in his case it's actually because he really should take better care of his teeth.

There is a long running tally of questions stored at the base of his skull, new ones constantly being added as old ones are (satisfactorily or not) answered or forgotten. He is not looking for answers so much as people with similar questions.

Brought back from his reverie by something, he finds himself sitting. Two hands cradle the hot white cup of coffee. Now one hand is scratching his chest and the parts of his back it can reach. Setting the coffee on the floor, stretching, taking up the coffee again and moving to the window frame, he inspects the dew collecting on the paint, watches the little rivulets form as the dew drops reach that point when they can no longer act immune to gravity. He had resolved to quit drinking and he had meant it. Today will be the start of something new. Finish the rest of the bottle (a paltry amount to let go to waste when the future holds none, ever again.) and that will be that. Church mouse and judge and all that from now on. Walking slowly to the table, gently lifting and removing the cap to peer down the barrel at its remnants, he feels a little blooming joy in his heart to see the orange/brown liquid and catch its burning wafted vapor in his sleep crust nostril.

The bottle is gone. As is the coffee and there are things to be done. Should he save this last bottle to display? Empty and proud, a trophy of self control and temperance? A shrine to his inner teeto-taler, kept locked away for so many years, now given the chance to shine gloriously? For the world will come knocking. Battering down the door to catch a glimpse. New horizons will shine, opportunities present themselves. He smiles, stirring yesterdays wet grounds in the filter. Running the coffee maker the first time through the recycled grounds, then refilling the tank with the first brew to run it through a second time, hopefully making something resembling a normal cup of coffee. He's never sure how well this works but has been doing it for years, and will probably continue to.

Someone kicks the neighbors wall and a doorbell slips through the floor. Opening his eyes to find everything washed in colors of sunset. The book he had dozed off to closed around his thumb. After his morning rebirth into sobriety, he took some laundry down to the machines and came back up to finish White Tiger by Aravind Adi-ga. Scanning backwards over a few pages before his sweaty thumb print, finding the last passage that seems familiar, he dog-ear's the corner and props himself up.

Heading down to check on his clothes, knowing that having dozed for so long someone will have tampered with them. Sure enough, they're piled in a dirty corner of the floor. Seeping and soaking in their own wetness where they'd been hefted. Leaving them for a moment like a sulking child, he steps outside and lights a cigarette. Watching the smoke and the ember. Tasting the hot acidic tobacco. Eyelids droop, head back, leaning against the wall. Exhale. Inhale. Repeat.

Slowly tearing all the lightning and dark and empty ruins of sketches out of books and off walls and out of eyes and rolling them under an arm, some smashed and bent at the middle or edges of their roll, some dangling unrolled or only partially, walk into the streets of weather like upstate NY surrounded by New Orleans styled plantations and graveyard silence on the days when there are no parades. The sky was wrapped in cracking leather and twine and it sagged and dripped under the lake it struggled to contain. Walk. Although dressed for the elements I had brought no boat and began to sink into the street which, by now, was nothing more than slushy asphalt and mire. The bottoms of the papers moistened and began to soak up in patterns of debris and rot and when, up to nipples in sinking, I let them unfurl into the sky, I loved what they had become.

Paper and styrofoam coffee cups, their spaceship lids liver spotted, cling to the table. Sprouting up between ash trays, cigarette packs, lighters, a box of generic cheese its, unused coasters with Thai beer brands; Chang, tsing ha, folded squares of wax paper, stereo remote, the edges of bills their bulk smothered under the weight of stacked plates, bound together by the blood of forsaken meals. A microcosm birds eye view of Los Angeles. It's crooked pathways, stained crumpled facades stamped with old news, pushing together, fighting for space, piling up to the verge of collapse.

He is eating mixed greek olives from a jar. These particular ones, he expects, are not actually from Greece. The Ralphs Private Select brand being his prime source of suspicion. Hoping though, despite all the turmoil facing that island, that someone is tending to the olive trees. Or is it bushes? No, it's trees. Right?

His wandering footsteps place erratic prints upon the floor in the form of an intricate dance. The heavy gauge black plastic of the trash bag sliding, skipping, jittery across the short carpet hairs as he drags the bulging sack behind him. Wanting to rid himself of whatever is not bolted down. Once a week, or more realistically, every two months, he does a reasonably deep clean of the apt. Like everything in life, he's put it off longer than he should, and, now that it's done, a feeling of lightness, a settling calm has found him in the empty clean spaces. Each time, deciding that he will, vowing even, stay more on top of these things. Removing physical clutter, or negating it's onslaught, could diminish the emotional draining, the imperceptible tangles lurking in his days and nights. He will try to remember this.

We listen to sirens our whole life, he thinks, one passing below, stuttering before finding its voice and whooping a clear, circular song down Beverly. Some close, some farther away, all bound for us eventually. Each time, every day, all day, the busy drivers of the Schaefer Ambulance Company, with a bloop, a wail, the wheezing explosive honk of an airhorn, decry their flight, a sort of inverse Paul Revere on the trail of death.

He can remember the story of a girl from his home town. A girl, someone's friend or sister or cousin, battling depression, schizophrenia, battling a world full of confused onlookers that wouldn't, couldn't understand. Voices pulling from every direction, never sure where reality began and ended. 'Till one day, in the back of an ambulance, just as it hit full speed on the freeway, the voices gently slipped her skinny wrists from the thick canvas restraints, quietly distracted the medic, and she, like a cartoon floating on a stream of delicious scent, stepped weightless out the back doors into the reality of tumbling bloody death at 65+ mph.

Most days Paul wonders if he's crazy. Standing here, his little apartment, little dreams, little understanding of how to act, how to know if he knows what he wants, what he is doing, where he is going. If some day soon those sirens will be coming for him. Wishing someone would tell him now if they are. Somebody whose opinion he trusts. Just to know. To take precautionary measures. Or maybe it can't be a person with a trusted opinion. Maybe his craziness is reflected in every John and Jane he knows, of which the numbers are dwindling. But who can be sure. He's always been crazy to someone. What if there're right? What if he's right? An entire planet of lunatics. Kings to priests presidents thieves scientist prostitutes bus boy bank teller junkie teacher cop liquor store attendant mad as hatters. One deranged mob hierarchy basking in the glow of a dying star.

Who then are *they* to determine his sanity? And what if he is crazy? He's not violent. Or, hasn't been since he was much younger. When he thought he could win the approval of the world by taking the hardest punch, drinking the most liquor without a mixer, berating young neo-nazis while pulling from a bottle of Jack till they dropped him or, he and whoever he was with were thrown out of the party. So he is no longer a danger to others, mostly. What does it matter then if he is crazy? He just has to find a way to let his chaos work for him. Some way to monetize his actions, leaving him and his ideas to wander freely. $20,000 a year is shit if you hate your job, but, if he could make that in an environment where he was free to be himself, he'd consider it a win.

He has been waiting for a moment to exist. Waiting for the world to catch up, to understand him. Each time he thinks about the reality of himself as he appears to others, he feels sick. Wondering at the fine line between perception and action. If people misunderstand, misinterpret him, at what point does that become his responsibility? To some people he will always be different than he sees himself. That's ok. They don't have the benefit of his inner monologue. But, he must ask himself, if he is perceived, he is perceived through his actions, the things he does and says and at what point must he reevaluate his actions?

Should he change so that the outside world views him as he does himself? If he does so, will his inner dialogues change? Will this be selling out, pandering, an attempt at normalcy that will rob him of creativity, individuality, and self respect? Will he become another cog in the droning mechanism of vapid commerce?

A car alarm masturbatorially mimics the ambulance. He ties the bulging bag and sets it in front of the door. Knowing he needs to place things directly in his path, needs to trip over things to remember them.

Looking left and right, turning to see from where I had come, I continue walking. My vision reaches across a long low basin, oblong and searching, stretching out short ways before me. There is a concrete path I keep on my right, feet moving through the grass, following up and forward to where it crests the rim of the basin and disappears down toward the other side's forever. Great red oxidized steel structures; silos and pipes, curling tubes with cutoff valves 3' in diameter, some standing alone, isolated, keeping watch, the others, huddled in groups, watching the watchers or ignoring them. I can sense they are captive, as are their captors. I alone am free to move. And the trees, elms or sycamores maybe. I know they are not pines. Everyone knows they aren't pines. Their thin knotted branches clang and whip against the steel, competing to be heard over the growing of the grass. The grass; thin, long and wispy that you see on the american plains and in movies where a man and woman run toward each other in dreams, one often disappearing before the other can reach them. There are no birds or rabbits, no evidence of any mammals, but I am positive there are mice. Small white or grey mice darting in and out of the dirt and grass living off whatever mice eat, drinking at some small oasis that only mice know about. I have felt the gradual incline for some time, the ground rising up under my feet, but the ridge remains painted, neither larger nor smaller, far away. I notice, for the first time, the hazy purple mountains with grey white caps to the west. Distance always subdues with purples, I think. For no reason at all I assume I am headed north. There is light, it is light out, but I can find no sun, no focal point for the brightness. The grass is getting shorter and the steel guardians of the basin grow taller, skinnier and more infrequent. The clang bang of the trees wailing for approval or freedom, fading. Their long legs holding down the earth against wind and rain and sleet and snow keep them from continuing with me. They are the postmen of this valley. I am at the top of the rim and, to my surprise, it does not drop again but continues, flat and level. Stepping now onto the path I head to the great picture of a city before me, isolated as an island which grew up from the earth, built by the tiny hands of man. Small men with dreams of tower steel and glass that would rise high enough to reflect the clouds and the sun. Mirrored facades that would look into each others eyes and compete for superiority, strength, height, beauty or purpose. Buildings built so tall that men were hired to build things big enough to build these silver dreams. I wonder how often a man enters the building he has helped construct. What good is a board room to a construction worker? I am closing in on the city. The air has become noticeably thicker and, stopping to listen, I can feel a faint shake and roll beneath my feet and hear the promise of movement. Like a lover trying discreetly to exit the bed, to meet the day or escape without waking you. It is on top of me. All around and up as far as they eye can see; cars and signs, pasty neon waiting for night to shine, people and places and things, the asphalt in the streets sparkling with dust like confetti and the cars that pick it up and push it to the walls and the sky and into my heart. Honk, yell, speak, no one will hear you, this I know. The streetlights have no powers here and the people are blind using briefcases as bicycles and canes as mustaches and machetes to chop poke swing their way forward. No one ever looks back. The only thing back there is what you've left behind. Realizing all this, I see myself in the mirrored door of a glass bagel shop, my hand meeting my hand on the glass and pushing through me to enter. The bell rings and I look up to watch it dance and die. An old man sits at a chipped marble counter in tortoise shell horn rimmed glasses and a brown wool trench coat. He's being held in place by a hat thats just a little too big for what I picture as a pointy balding head. Drinking his coffee and smoking his cheroot, the smell of both lingers and mixes with the bread and the yeast and the clamor of the kitchen. A whiff of grease cutter. I can tell he's hard and worn and gentle. For a moment he becomes a snub nose revolver with an short thin line of whipped cream laying along the top of the barrel, then he is just the old man again. I've been in old Mex. He says. On a religious quest, a spiritual journey. Looking for the wonder and the lack and the end. How'd it go? The man sips his coffee and adjusts his glasses with the middle finger of his left hand. Well enough, as far as religious quests go. Only the wounded died. Hearts were broken and I found no answers, but we're all just kidding ourselves if we expect to. But you've got to fake it 'till you make it as they say. I ordered coffee, taking off a jacket I hadn't meant to be wearing, draping it over the back of the stool.. You can tell a lot from a man by his eyes. His sexual proclivities his moral aptitude. You saw an old stray dog when you walked in, maybe you didn't know it, regardless, old men have a tendency to ramble, and you sat down and let me talk., listening intently and I see no judgment in your eyes. I will grant you one wish and if I can make it happen, it'll happen.

There's nothing left of the money he'd saved. Well, three hundred bucks, which is just enough for nothing. Unsure of where it's all gone. He has a notion of course, but things haven't quite coalesced the way he'd vaguely imagined they would. This far in, he'd assumed he would have found a community, a sense of direction, would have assimilated some of the creative spark pulsing through the city and tuned it, honed it's energy to a point, harnessed it's history as a means of propulsion. Instead, he feels, after these few long months, like he's just arrived. Or really, like he's nowhere yet. The grids of pavement and street signs still foggy, still a jumble, a piled mash of spaghetti brain.

Yesterday, pausing from combing the job ads on craigslist, he cut a destined to bounce rent check and headed down to the managers office. It was late in the day, late enough, he hoped, that the building manager would have locked the door and headed up to her fifth floor apartment. It would take her some time to get around to the deposit after her usual cursory glance at the check. He didn't want to short her, just needed some time. Buy a coupl'a days and make it seem like a mistake.

He'd done the same at a bank once, back in more youthful days he tries not to long for. Just a little loan. Write a deposit slip for twice the amount you need, a reasonable sum of course, then withdraw the half that's immediately released. He hadn't had time to pay the bank back, they'd caught on pretty quick. Or maybe he'd been a little slow at getting around to the deposit. Either way they got their money and closed his account to boot. Hoping for better luck this time as he slid the envelope under the door. Besides, they had recently replaced the toilets in every unit but his, leaving him without water for a day, barging in with toilet in tow before informing him that the new commode was too big for the space, leaving the old one, chipped and dusty. He should be getting a break on the rent for that.

He sent off about 200 applications before getting a single reply. A carpet cleaning company in Santa Monica. Needing something, anything, before things come to a grinding halt, he googles the address and covering his tattoos with a long sleeve shirt and tie, heads out early morning on vigilant tiptoe, hoping to avoid landlady detection, gliding the two hour bus with one change to Santa Monica and the interview for a job he doesn't want.

In the small waiting room of an industrial complex, keeping himself occupied until the manager makes himself available by studying the booklets on carpet care, looking at swatches of befores and afters, until a square gruff man with powerful arms calls him into a small square office. There are two square chairs on either side of a square wooden desk. Square frames hang along the walls with square matting and square pictures. The man keeps his gray hair cut in the "high and tight" fashion of the military, giving even his head the shape of a… Paul is overwhelmed by the geometry of it all.

They talk about previous experience, future plans, Paul feeding his best lines of working stiff BS and trying to seem like an asset. On the bus back to K-town he feels like it'd gone well, but by the time he gets home he's having second thoughts about the commute. Hours later, the sun has withered and he's still poking around the glowing lists of jobs. Tweaking his resume to fit anything from personal assistant to web design to warehouse manager to construction worker.

PA jobs are mostly out of the question since they all seem to require a vehicle, as do many of the construction jobs in addition to having your own tools, but he does apply to one delivery job with little information offered, save it's a deli, it's close, and they have their own vehicle. After some preliminaries over email, they request the submission of a driving record. He coughs up the $2 to get one on the DMV website and is pleased to find out it's not as bad as he expected. He's even more surprised the following day when he receives a call from the monotone manager of the establishment, suggesting an interview.

Hey Mr. Paul!

John barely glances from the small screen that broadcasts a Dodger game behind the thick scratched bulletproof glass at Saver Liquor. He sets the usual fifth of Jim Beam on the counter as Paul returns the greeting, adding that he'll only need a pint tonight.

Whatcha, wanna take it easy for once? He smiles at Paul, turning in time to shout profanities at whatever has just happened to the Dodgers.

Big interview tomorrow, Paul replies, glad to be able to say so (even if it's not a BIG interview). He's long suspected that John, who works every day, wonders what the hell this white boy does that he can be buying liquor and drinking it at all hours of the day and night. John probably doesn't think of him at all he realizes.

These fucking guys. Can you believe it? What'd you say?

Job interview.

Oh Heeeyyyy. Good luck then. He replaces the fifth with a pint.

Thanks. 'Night John. The sound of traffic swallows another slew of expletives and Paul moves through the electric bell and back across Berendo to the Dicksboro.

Putting on his interview clothes, the only ones fit for such an occasion, trying to knot the tie in such a way that it hangs over a faded splotch on the shirt that had appeared at some point, reflecting on a time when he'd had several suits, one with three pieces even, and a few ties to choose from. Not that any of the suits were expensive, or even of a decent quality, but he'd had them. And not that he wants or needs suits, he doesn't, except for today, but he wonders where they've gone. He has an aptitude for losing clothes. But, more oddly, also for gaining them without purchase or notice (One of his most comfortable shirts is grey, with NEIL printed across the chest. He doesn't know where it came from or which Neil is being referred to, but it is comfortable and there are several Neil's that he likes). He's disrobed his upper half again, worried about splattering toothpaste on his few remaining articles of professional/funeral/wedding/other things he's never invited to attire.

Thinking about those suits makes him think about the job he'd had them for. Brushing away the dry whiskey breath, sun throwing undulating shadows of shower curtain breeze around the bathroom. That was the year he'd had three jobs at once. A/V Tech for a hoity-toity hotel, Blockbuster Video, and warehouse schlepping. Three jobs and plenty of time and youthful vigor to drink and wile away the short hours of night. He'd figured once that he made fifty grand that year, between those jobs, and he couldn't remember having spent any more or less money than he ever did. 50k. Twice as much as he'd ever made before or since, and still, at the beginning or end of every month it'd been a struggle. Money has always been like socks to Paul, nice when new, but soon enough a bunch of singles, then altogether gone.

He's finished re-knotting the tie, forgetting about the spot, pat checking his pockets; keys, lighter, smokes, wallet, bus fare, inhaler, phone, chapstick, and hits the streets just in time to dart through traffic and onto the 14 bus west. Taking a seat in back where he can stretch his legs out, resting them on the silver bar anchoring the side facing seats ahead, slouching low and staring at passing buildings, or, more accurately, the stationary buildings he rumbles past, when he realizes he's forgotten a resume. He had twenty at home, printed and sandwiched in the book he also forgot. His hand sweats absently clenched. Paul sees the sweaty hand clutching a resume. He is not utterly lost in the world. Only mostly lost, with bright spots of luck/ chance/fate/divine intervention, things he tries to keep out of the way of, powers buried deep within him, or existing far beyond him. He will let them work, trying to help out where he can.

At Fairfax he takes the 217 towards Hollywood, smoking half a cigarette on the bus bench waiting. It's around 5 as he steps out on Sunset, re-lighting the cigarette and watching the comings and goings, the still faint neon working slowly toward vibrancy. Buying a pack of gum, one of those 25cent packs, he chews a stick and checks himself in the mirrored glass of the gas station. Pleased with his moderately upstanding reflection.

How could there be so much about this person that he does not know? There doesn't seem to be any story, no linear set of events, that have created the character he sees in the reflection. The character others know as Paul. There is only a series of decisions, none of which ever seemed to be within his control. Opportunities, for lack of a better term, only ever arising at the end of a fuse. Everything he'd ever consciously yearned for started with great intention, with the highest of hopes, all endlessly sputtering to an unforeseeable end, vastly different from the original design.

Approaching the chipped brick building with its thickly varnished pioneer-theme-park-brown wood, the gold leaf lettering in classic old timey font, he ditches the gum in an overflowing trash can, pulling the loose brass ornamented handle of the door and stepping into that early 1900's flavor of old Hollywood. The air close, marinating pungent with slow cooking flesh, stewing with soups and hot breads thick with bubbling cheese. Moving over uneven tiles toward a woman lolling behind a register. Standing there, taking in the wood, the brass, the tarnished ornate details, the piles, pyramids, rowed bottles of wine and spirits by the thousands. The woman reaches above, taking down a glass, casually leaning on her shoulder and pulling wine from one of a series of taps behind the counter before handing the glass to a cute waitress who bolts up the stairs, two at a time, without spilling a drop.

Hi. I have a 5:30 interview. I'm Paul.

Someone will be right with you. Behind the counter she picks up a phone and announces him, presumably to the monotone man he'd spoken with the previous evening.

Wandering the small floor plan he feels the acute foreignness of this environment, a surreal vibe that links him, almost, to this landscape in the way that he could, if everything goes well, find himself standing in this same place, off and on, for the foreseeable future. The same dis/connected feeling from the carpet cleaners waiting room, from all the previous places he's waited for interviews or first days on the job. The new surroundings, and his brain wondering how they will feel if/when they become commonplace. Once he forgot how crazy and foreign it had all seemed at this time.

It bothers him that, if everything goes well, this will be his triumph. He has no qualms about working for a living, he can tell himself that this will be a good story, these situations, a small and brief step in the series of events that will eventually lead him to greatness, or happiness or whatever. None the less, it's worrisome, in the present, that his hopes rest here. That this quaint monument to a bygone era may be the key to his immediate sanity.

He is being escorted down a steep, winding thin basement staircase. The wood paneling of the walls is replaced by concrete block and the feeling in the air and mood change as he steps into a catacomb of dry goods. Cases of booze and coffee stacked head high, shelves full of tinned fish and meat, piles of slouched, runny newsprint. In the monotone managers office at the far corner of the tomb, the door closes, their conversation cut off to the world, alone with another person who is alone with him, it's like every other interview he's ever had. Work experience, goals, strengths and weaknesses, the tired list of innocuous questionnaire frivolities. He knows this man is sizing him up. Of course he is. That is the point of an interview. Watching his movements from behind the desk piled with papers and ledgers, magazines about wine, a guidebook to the bordeaux wine country, various bottles of spirits at varying levels of tasted, and right in front of Paul, on the edge of the desk, a small metal toy train set. He's answering a question but is imagining the middle aged man alone, late night, several fingers in to one of the bottles, sitting crosslegged on the floor, mouth full of chug-a-lugs and choo-choos.

He doesn't think about it now, too busy playing a character, but later he'll wonder why, in these situations, he always feels the need to put on a good face, to say the right thing at the right time, to sell himself. He never dares to ask too many questions. Never feels he has the right, or if he does, can't bring himself to extend this charade any longer, to ask what things will be done for him. What is this guys previous experience? What are his weaknesses? Why is he, Paul, always so desperate by the time he starts looking for a new job that he can't afford to find one that fits him, rather than the other way around?

They shake hands and the monotone manager, telling him he'll hear something in a day or two, escorts him as far as the office door, which promptly closes behind him. Back at the top of the stairs, surveying the various employees busy about their tasks, oblivious to him as anything other than an obstacle in their clockwork choreographed routines, casting a glance at each one just long enough to wonder at what a daily interaction with this person would be like.

Just as he's about to leave, as a token of good faith, he plops a bottle of $3 red and a fifth of whiskey on the counter to drink in the back of the bus. The girl behind the counter seems not to register any memory of him as she rings up the booze and stepping out onto now dark Sunset, rounding a corner, he cracks the whiskey, absorbing it essence, equalizing his aura with the glowing coal powered buzz of the strip.

Black night shadows feel welcoming as they pale toward blue for sunrise. The blinding yellow stucco of El Salvadorian bakeries has yet to overwhelm ocular sensibilities. Lighting a cigarette, he listens over light traffic to the paper catching flame as it trembles on his lip. Somewhere up Vermont a pale bell tolls but he can never remember how to read the legato punctures. Is it one for every hour? But he's never heard the toll more than eight times.

On these early mornings he'll find himself out on the sidewalk. Standing amid the pulsing, the rushing wind system created by passing cars that whip by, engines groaning as they race down the blvd. He is watching a short, round, latino woman at the bus stop. Watching her fuss over a child in a pink stroller, the chapped sun-bleached handles laden with bags, trying alternately to quiet the crying with toys or pacifier. Trying to pacify.

He is waiting for the call he is sure will come. Last nights interview was nothing special, there were no overt signs that he'd clenched it, but, for some reason, he feels as though it's a sure thing. Feel the easing tension inside, as if he is already behind the wheel of that van, cash in hand. He should probably be upstairs hunched in front of the computer, remodeling & resending his resume. Instead, he takes another sip of Tecate in the shade, watching the woman and child maneuvering up the beeping ramp onto the bus.

Antonio pushes an overflowing cart, the contents of which seem to be some passed out, or at least uncomfortably immobile, companion. The sound of hard rubber wheels bumping over sidewalk cracks and the jangling metal of their vibration overtakes Pauls reverie and replaces it with dread. This development threatens to endanger his momentary calm. But does it? He tries to believe in himself, to believe there is goodness inside him as he raises a hand and waves.

Going unnoticed as they clang past, echoing down Beverly. His mind, vigilant in it's struggle to continually seek out worry, switches from dread of the encounter to narcissistic, or maybe, hopefully, it's self exploratory, criticism of what his initial reaction says about the kind of person he is. As the bus pulls toward him, he forgets about the empties potted in the planter, sliding aboard through closing doors, almost missing a hand hold as they jolt forward, feeding quarters into the fare machine.

Taking a seat at the only open window, looking out, the grinning face of Antonio passing by. A flood of images and emotions boil up. He is overwhelmed by the empty pain of humanity. The chance and struggle of it all. Am I strong enough to endure life, he wonders. When every possible thing could potentially go wrong, is going wrong, somewhere, to someone, right now? Things must be going wrong for Antonio. And what if that was me? Could I endure? Could I conquer? I would surely have to rely on the goodness of my fellow man. Much more even, than I do now. What if I find myself in those shoes. Will I remember the times I've felt like I wanted all those needy people to leave me alone? And if I do, will I be able to beg for the support of others, support I was often reluctant or unwilling to give? Will I look at my dirty hands and see the hands I tried not to touch as I dropped change from a distance too great for germs to travel through?

Real, deep fear, rips through his guts, choking, nearly causing him to vomit. Coughing and struggling to breathe, tears magnify the corners of his eyes as he dives into the backpack for a beer and begins to chug. The few heads that have turned to wonder, shoot back forward once he's composed himself enough to look around. He would laugh if he could, about what he is or isn't, will or won't be. Looking out the window again, there is no Antonio. Still, there is the faded specter of that dirty, smiling face.

Looking around, left, right, in the rearview mirrors. Taking an airplane bottle of whiskey from the pocket of his apron and downing it, putting the empty in the center console and shifting the car into gear. Headed up Laurel Canyon, this early, before the marine layer's burnt off, he has a sense of hurtling toward opportunities unknown. The delivery van, wide and low, hugging the corners, shifting down into second, the fuzzy sharp pin pricks of Lowell Fulson's guitar, the wrung out tension and the heart pumping beat flying out the open windows and fading on the skins of trees, plants, squirrels, eaten up in the mechanical drone of gardeners, bouncing off the painted metal epidermis of cars. Lighting a cigarette, trying to keep the ash contained anywhere outside the vehicle in an effort to prevent another haranguing from the monotone boss.

Double parking on a steep grade down the street from the address on the handscrawled delivery slip, he sets the e-brake and punches up the hazards. Another airplane emptied whiskey. Drink from the bottle. Taking a pickle from the bag and eating it, replacing the others. Light a cigarette and walk up the hill. No wonder these people never leave their god damn homes. Huffing, puffing, worried the paper handles on the paper bags will snap under the weight of the bulging, steaming jewish food as they are so prone to do.

Snuffing out the cigarette at the brick driveway and putting it in his back pocket, he bends to check the contents of the bags, having forgotten to do so earlier, and lucky for him everything's there. It's the worst when shit's missing or the order is otherwise fucked up. It means having to tell the customer you'd forgotten to check. Or say nothing. Hope they say nothing, forget to check, or don't realize until after you've left. He can take it off the bill or expect a lesser tip. Go back to the shop. Pretend not to understand. Blame someone else. Take responsibility. Get behind in deliveries. Get reprimanded. Get a big tip and feel bad about it. Get a big tip and fuck 'em I deserve it.

In the end, knowing he is to blame for his own inconvenience, if the customer, the monotone manager, fellow employees, are understanding or give him a hard time, they're right. He is often half-hearted, haphazard, not wholly conscious, or daydreaming and finds it difficult not to label himself the victim. Always catching the hard breaks, fingers worked to the bone, all the other bullshit excuses he gives himself about why poor ol' Paul has it so goddamn hard.

But he knows this is bullshit. Powerful bullshit, but bullshit none-the-less. That seductive lure, the problem solving inaction of blame that takes away all fear of failure to the tune of never stood a chance. But it's tough to take it all in stride. And Paul doesn't even have much to take. He wants to learn to ease his self reproach without letting BS slide. To be understanding of his own shortcomings but wary of their existence.

Counting the cash he has on hand, with $70 to go back in the register, he's made a lousy 8 bucks so far. He'll need a few regulars, big tippers, not these housekeepers who are afraid or not authorized to tip. Blowing into his cupped hand in an attempt to check his breath, coming up undecided with a hint of pickle, he knocks at the door. After two minutes and a few more knocks he finds the doorbell, strategically hidden by a large sap-sticky plant, gives a ring and then a holler. Delivery! Walking to the large front window he tries to catch any shadow of life through the heavy drapes. Just as his face gets close enough to fog the glass, the door opens and a woman lets out a loud, venomous—Finally.

At the estuary of Selma & Sunset, leaving the van running at the curb, he steps into the Liquor Locker, 4 more airplanes (I don't care if it is 98¢, who buys fireball? No one, the clerk replies) of Evan Williams, some mints, and 2 of those little gummy hamburgers that'll rip your molars out if they're stale. Breakfast. Tomorrow he'll go to the store and buy some real food. Fruits, vegetables, a chicken, and he'll have to quit drinking all this shit again. Get some solid grub in him and leech out the booze. The other way around.

Downing two of the airplanes as proof of the seriousness of this last hurrah, driving the back streets and stop sign littered residentials to the shop. If he drinks enough today, it will prove that he is serious about quitting tomorrow. Sound and oft repeated logic that has been met for many years with immediate success, followed shortly by failure.

Looking at the line of bags, ready and waiting to be shuttled around Hollywood, trying to figure out the best order of delivery based on seniority v. surliness of recipient, distance of travel and most potential for tip. Loading the bags into the back of the van, feeling that slow disjointedness slipping in. He's been taking too much time and things have gotten backed up. He'll have to step it up on the work and slow it down on the whiskey or he'll never make noon. Pouring a to-go cupajoe, up the slick wooden stairs to the parking lot where he eases into the lowslung driver's seat, gushing out into the stream of traffic on the boulevard, colliding into the sighing motors, shouting horns, the tumbleweed figures panning for gold at street corners and stoplights.

It's a long ride back to town in shattering quiet. He was listening to the local classical station before it went to static, the voice of some holly roller bleating through in escalating increments, a fuzzed out mix of Brahms and the wrath of god. He shuts it off. Somewhere out in Benedict Canyon, sitting at a stoplight, watching a leaf fall in slow motion through his headlights. Big and pale green rumpled, he can see the furry hairs reflected in the lights before it disappears beneath the hood and out of view.

He's thinking about a girl. She was quirky and always laughing or very sad and distant like a girl from 60's french cinema. Her hair was long and so was she. She showed him films he wasn't ready to see yet and he taught her to dance with a hat on. Now he wonders if she was ever those things at all. If she was anything of the dream he remembers, or if the filter of nostalgia, the feeling of the unresolved, hatched and grown strong with time, an opportunity unrealized, the onethatgotaway, enhances the spectrum of his memory.

From his right blind spot, an ambulance slowly pulls onto the street, red and white squatty fat man diving through the night. The lights turn on but there are no sirens and the driver refuses to pick up speed. The streets are empty. Paul drives slowly behind. It fakes left as if to make the turn then continues on around the long bending curve to the right, lights playing for the mist and the slick black streets like a coral snake, before darting out of sight.

He knows it will be waiting for him when the elbow in the road spits him out the other side. He can feel it's presence as he accelerates, letting gravity go to work on the pedal. Coming out of the turn the fat man is there, lights off, putting on speed and coming toward him. The lights and the coral snake once more. By the time they pass each other the ambulance is flying. Paul watches the misty halos landing on the faces of front yards, flinging duochrome vignette in 360degrees that vanishes black in a blink. Pulling over to watch in the rearview as they crest a hill and disappear. He wonders how long he can sit here before going back to work.

Coming up on midnight he steps out into the street, his face glows an old-irish-nose-red under the singing sign of The Golden Gopher on 8th Street. He's finished his drinks and, making a right on Olive, heads to 7th and the bus home. A tattered old woman stumbles toward him on spindly sea legs. The bus stop outside an old flophouse. She calls him Jesus. Calls him Tom Hanks. Complains about the spics waiting for the bus, about how good she feels. Grabs his shoulder and leans in close, Paul feeling himself disappear as black teeth gnashing jagged silhouettes leer with mute faces down the canal of his spine.

Now walks a young girl. (They are a juxtaposition, these two women and he sees them as such.) Lavender neoprene shorts buried deep between her bruised and not bruised ass cheeks. She is a daze. Too young, too still beautiful for the sweaty wandering halls, the crumpled hides that coagulate here. Her wet brown hair, the clear, ass length raincoat, everything makes him think apparition. He is caught in her gaze, seeing her lips moving, thinks she is asking if he is alone.

Are you a local?

He says nothing.

You look like one of my friends. From Hollywood.

No, he reports.

Her introducing herself as Pleasure, sticking out her left hand for a soft, wet-awkward handshake.

What goes on in a person mind? A beautiful girl, to be in the Olive Hotel, to have fallen so quickly. Maybe she never had anywhere to fall from. Such sad, silent eyes, that give an impression of seeing, but seeing what?

She still has most of her good looks, seems almost healthy. But the bruises, the glazed desolation. Her outfit wouldn't get a second glance at a rave, nor does it in the building behind her, where the carpets are worn through by junkie comings and goings. What had happened, is happening, to this fraying girl Pleasure? What events have played what part in her landing here?

He doesn't really know how he hasn't ended up in a place like this himself. In awe of, potentially, how much time he has left where he might. How many things can go wrong in life, how many times he's blown it to some degree or other in the past, how he's really only gotten to this point with the support of others, how easy it is to suddenly be alone in the world, how when that time came, it'd be all on him, and what would he do then? He'd had nothing but luck thus far, no matter how often he's considered himself unlucky. To still be alive, employed, without a criminal record, and white. Life had been made pretty easy for him, so it only stands to reason that, with all his tempting fate, the rug would be pulled out soon enough. He's watched worse things happen to better people his whole life and he can't think of any reason he should be left standing at the end of whatever path he's on. So maybe it's only a matter of time. Push these thoughts from your mind. Headphones greet eardrums to the tune of The Magnetic Fields *Busby Berkley Dreams*. Something in the melody makes him realize that the bus has stopped running for the night. He turns toward 7th and Metro to glide underground.

How long do you have to look for something before it's lost? He's been tossing the room for nearly an hour. Upending furniture, moving piles from here to there and back, looking under and in and above things, combing through clothes clean and dirty, now just one mixed pile in the corner crawling to the ceiling. Now, looking at the amount of clothing, thinking he could have overlooked a pants pocket, a crumpled t-shirt, he starts in on it again, more carefully. As the mound in front of him dwindles, garments fly cartoonish, globbing up the wall of an opposite corner.

Looking for his glasses is harder without the aid of his glasses. Fuming. Blurs move indistinguishable. Shuffling feet to prevent a self inflicted crunch. This is the second time in as many months that he's lost his only pair of glasses. There are not so many rooms to look in. Dread swarms his gut. He can't afford to get yet another pair after maxing out his last credit card to get the ones he's presently searching for. Even if he could borrow the money from his folks, already dreading that phone call (borrow? and pay them back with what? when? fuck.), he needs them by tomorrow so he can see the goddamn road. Goddammit! Motherfucker. He can't deal with this shit right now.

Looking in the empty spaces for a breath of something strong. A few swigs from the cap-less bottle under a t-shirt in the kitchen. A few more. Make a series of calls that all go unanswered to bars fished from snippets of last nights memories. Suckling at the bottle wondering; why me? why now? Lying back down on the bed. Prying himself up. Lacing his shoes and moving toward out of the building. Re-treading places he isn't sure he'd been, places he might have gone, the habitual streets, squinting, cursing, already knowing it's a lost cause. Knowing that he'd taken them off to rub his face in some fucking bar, some bench or ledge under the palm trees, and left them in the confusion of his drowning brain.

He probably could have looked for longer, but after walking for two hours and stepping in and out of three of the closest bars, he headed home, stopping at Saver Liquor for a bottle of bourbon. On the edge of his bed he takes a deep swig, lights a cigarette and makes an attempt at centering himself. He hadn't realized 'til he'd looked in the first bartenders face; the eyes change and narrow as he told the man how he might have been here last night, how he might have left his glasses—just how humiliated he would feel.

Not that there was any recognition in the man's eyes, Paul was probably just projecting his own self loathing, but after that, at the other two bars, he'd omitted the backstory and simply asked if there was a pair of black prescription glasses in the lost and found. It bothers him that he felt humiliated. Shamed by his own hand. He can feel the booze crawling around now. Shame. He says it out loud and (sort of forced) laughs. He should be used to it by now. With as much time as they've spent together? He should see it coming and throw his arms wide to greet such an old and constant companion. After all, it is always in response to invitation. His actions seem almost to show a discontent with familiar humiliations and so continually work to dredge up new ways of exploring the genre.

Here he is. Mentally, trying to prepare for the phone call to his parents where he'll ask for money and they'll give it to him. But not without their questions. Questions they know the answers to but want to hear in his voice. He hates this game. Probably because he knows it is on him to stop it. On him to keep himself out of these situations. He wishes that, just once, there could be a legit reason for his needing something. This line of thought is currently to much to tackle, so he pushes it out and replaces it with a new one. If only I had money. The phone rings in the house he grew up in as his eyes wander the room he lives in now. He sees the empty bottles, the empty packs of cigarettes and the full ashtrays, but he doesn't think about how that money could have been better spent. He is steeling himself for the conversation. Thinking about how to make sure his speech isn't slurred. I was just thinking about you, his mother answers.

This morning, looking at the ordered clipboard list of deliveries in front of him, glad to see they're all regulars. Easy stuff for good bread. These next two hours will be bearable, good even. He'll enjoy himself, zooming or putt putt puttering around Hollywood, depending on traffic. Windows down, knowing he'll have some cash in hand by noon. With the best ones, there's only as much talk as the time it takes to write in a tip and sign your name. Then it's off! Bam! Music going, hot coffee in the cup holder. Moving. Usually back down a hill or up one. The perfect day would be three orders every two hours. This gives you enough time to make all three deliveries without rushing and by the time you get back to the shop, there's three more. No hangin' around trying to look busy. Or worse, being busy, there, with all those people and phones and bullshit.

Each morning it's the old grey wizard of Formosa. An ex-political man with the follicular cranial accessories of a medieval magician. He seems like a good guy through and through. Always a ten spot on the check. One of those few that invites Paul in, (not that he wants to be invited in everywhere) tries to treat him as a human. Once, he'd given him $20 to change a lightbulb in the hall. Every day a bagel or an egg salad sandwich on egg bread, 1/5 Grey Goose, 1/5 Martini & Rossi extra dry, a six pack of diet coke. Every day.

Grey beard being the strictly weed type, the booze is for his partner. The guy gets kidney stones every couple years. Blaming the brand or mix of booze. At which point he changes it up, till the stones make their move again. The guy's still alive & in love, so chalk it up as a win. Paul can sympathize with the intake, and is holding out for the same kind of luck.

There's the girls up off Las Alturas. With their tiny shorts & tiny dogs, wine and cigarettes. He can never tell how old they are. Two young (twenty's?), one older (?) (Maybe the mother?). The house overflowing with the sweet stink of pot, always drinking, occasionally a stout young stubbly guy in baggy clothes who seems to be funding the shindig. A weird family drug party kinda vibe. Not in a negative way though, but yeah, also in a kind of negative way. Up in the hills, driving through Nichols Cyn for half an hour, steadily climbing the zigzag ribbon of road, turning up the last steep stretch, tires skip tractionless on loose gravel, catch, climbing higher, knock at the door, yapping dogs flood out, more inside, only to be asked to go back down the mountain for a different brand of smoke. But they always tip well, or decent, and are easy to deal with in the way of people detached.

Mr. Ronson off Kirkwood. Perfect image of a male spinster. Small and delicate, flesh seemingly woven of liver spots. Paul thinks he used to be a dancer. A choreographer. At the top of his game he fucked all the girls, all the boys. Now he drinks his vodka, perched, smoking his cigarettes with his dog in the musky bright natural light front room of a house dangling from the side of a mountain. All green and spreading out expanses at his feet, he seems holed up, hidden from the world. His television. His dog. Delivery charge accounts and $3 dollar tips. Every time, Paul holds the dogs leash while it pisses on a doorstep cactus, shaky Mr. Ronson signing the receipt. He's one of the good ones too. Pleasant & soft & sad.

Paul wonders, but never asks about his life. He never asks the people that really interest him. Afraid to upset the balance. Most people start yakin' their game pretty quick and, worried about starting to dislike the few enjoyable customers, he mostly lets things lay in the easiest possible manner.

Back at the shop he's surprised by the quiet. Servers stand in groups, looking over lines, weighing the merits of one acting class v. another. He'll have to find a way to keep busy. Or to keep looking busy. Hoping the phone will ring, an errand need running, anything to get him out of here, behind the wheel, moving.

Wiping condensation off the glass with a soggy clump of white paper towel, blue smell of windex on his tongue. The double panes dirty on the inside. Impossible, after all these years as a cooler in constant use, to get looking clean. Creeping of dirt congruent with time. Fronting bottles. The deli humming quiet as the glass case around him. Clang. Paul knows if he can master these small tasks as an art, find momentary purposefulness in each windshield wiper swipe of his arm, everything will be fine. He often finds himself in the middle of a daydream, a dream about taking things more slowly, chewing food longer or savoring tea and listening to a record each morning, looking at daily chores as opportunities for meditation on clutter-less living.

Reminded now of the way it feels - shitty morning hangover,

your guts all tied up and gargling, head continuous slamming pain of the brain as a raw leaking gash, deep loathing, the immediate tranquility of a first drink, the ensuing statistically measurable gains toward wholeness with each ensuing drink— all going blackout haywire eventually, but those measured gains, that moment of completeness captured fleeting— there aught to be a way to seize that same feeling in every action. In a lasting way. To, at least, prolong the median levels of calm and decrease the duration and frequency of the dips. With practice of course. He knows there is no revelation that can get him there instantly, overnight, questions answered, contentedness on lock down, but he thinks, hopes, that maybe this idea of a more meditative lifestyle is a part of the answer.

The problem with Paul is that, spending so many hours with himself, dissecting, exploring, wondering, dragging himself over the coals, dusting off, standing again atop a self erected pedestal, he often has such revelations, sure that he has finally hit upon the answer. And, so applying himself, often times not enough, towards some new practice, it is quickly abandoned after dismal signs of progress. Somewhere in the back of his mind he must know that there is no one sure answer, that the world is not one problem with one solution, but more a series of problems, sometimes concurrently, that require different modes, different tactical approaches, to conquer . Even these words; problems & conquer, maybe there is an advantage to dismissing these adjectives in describing life. A problem is a description of a situation/choice in a moment, given a negative connotation. To ascribe conquer as a positive triumph over the situation, prescribes negativity to said situation where none was needed, creating a problem.

He is lucky to be alive. Knowing this, as he does, and being emotionally connected to this knowledge are two different things. What is he supposed to do with this information? It does not buoy his spirits to know that he should be dead and is not, nor does it bring him any consolation that death is always lingering, our collective fate. He sometimes wishes he'd been aborted, like all his attempts at living. Never given the chance to waste the air, food and water that could have been used to sustain a better, more splendid, grateful being, more useful to the world than the swollen sack of lazy shit that confronts him in every mirror and window, that needles him with every thought.

But he is too cowardly or stupid to end it. Maybe he is just waiting, like he does with everything else, for something to happen. For Mars to align with Saturn, for Hope to intercede on his behalf, for something or anything to give meaning to his slogging existence.

All this thinking in his head. This is his comfort zone. But is it? It is for sure the place he spends most of his time. The question of his comfort, with he, himself, is debatable. Sometimes it is violent here or helplessly confused, the streets are mean, or there is a jumble of Calcutta traffic where thoughts fly along unmarked paths, missing each other or colliding, continuing on or falling dead. It can be blank and empty, or full of trinkets, but it is rarely ever peaceful. He would visit such an establishment infrequently if it were built of brick and mortar, outside of him. What if everything that makes sense only makes sense to me? What if no one, anywhere, ever, agrees with me? Two girls laugh and he wonders if they are laughing at or with him. Is he laughing? No. He's even sure he isn't being weird. Not on the outside at least. He decides to stop thinking and lose himself in his work. Concentrate on breathing. Body awareness. Watching the cloud of overspray windex drift elegantly across the glass.

What, does it really matter if he is misunderstood? Maybe he can operate and continue in the world without anyone ever appreciating his perspective. We're all trying to do something that's never been done before; to live our lives, individual and unique as they are, successfully. But Paul is no great philosopher or parable writer, he's more of a fortune cookie editor, a bathroom graffiti-er. He steps to the side, allowing a customer to grab a root beer.

Flipping through bags of chips, checking dates and replacing the expired bags, it feels good to be doing his job. To have a job to do and be doing it. Nothing else to do in this moment but look at the expiration date on chips. There is nothing really wrong here. He is no closer and no further away from truth. Conventional wisdom dictates that, at the moment of death, unedited film of life playing, you won't want to see too many scenes examining BBQ chips and expiration dates, but the argument he is making to he is that, in those scenes, what's really more important is the underlying emotion of the character i.e. himself. He can't quit this job right now. Not without sacrificing some of his standard of living (not that there is so much to sacrifice). And there might be something to the argument that, such a sacrifice, if it were directed toward a goal, could be beneficial. But what that direction would be? He isn't sure. So for now this is good enough.

His life is full of things he wants, and as many things he doesn't. But it will always be thus, until he learns to appreciate even the things he doesn't. In a minute he'll answer the phone, or help a customer, or some other thing that will unconsciously throw him for an emotional ringer, making him forget completely, and in fact, run headlong in the opposite direction of the breakthrough he's just had. And sometime later he'll remember this and feel foolish. But if he can increase the frequency of these thoughts while minimizing the negative, the hopeless and helpless, he'll be on a righter path than he was yesterday.

What are his relationships with these people, his coworkers? How do they see him interacting? Do they know that he isn't? Interacting. Just acting. There is no give and take. He takes nothing. Gives only what is required to keep from giving any more. They do not want his real. No one does. He is a good sounding board for their jokes, their moods, their bitching. A quiet but expressive face and a well placed word is all they need to continue their monologues. They are good people, full of passion, experience and life, but he cannot imagine a conversation that would continue if he expressed himself freely. He has one friend here and that's enough. Almost too much. But he needs one person who understands. Who knows what it's like to not be known.

It's an incredible work out to keep from being swept away in the kinetic chaotic current of it all. Working here at the deli for a few months now, with periods of drunk and sober, but mostly in between. When it's busy, tensions run high. Blame lays strewn about. The folks taking deliveries and answering phones blame traffic or holidays, the drivers blame traffic and the kitchen, the kitchen blames the customers. The monotone manager sits in the basement, surrounded by dusty bottles & yesterday's news, watching it all unfold in black & white security footage.

There is only one united front here, against the customers. The general consensus being that, if we could just be free of them, everything would be more enjoyable. Little cliques thrive. Who slept with who and lives with who else & fraternizes with which and when. Who was invited to beer & BBQ last weekend and what was gossiped about regarding whom. This is how it seems to him at least. This is why he remains outside, trying to exist as less than a memory. Most of the time. Occasionally falling prey to the nature of intimate space.

For years he'd seen it, in movies and books, the played out trope of struggling thespians slinging hash between auditions. Trying to make connections, networking. With sides for the next potential break taped to the inside cover of notepads. Studying, or pretending to. And somehow, everyone is from the midwest. And just like the celluloid and the stories about getting discovered at Schwab's promised, it seems like nearly every waiter/waitress in this city has a headshot and a reel and they're all shuttling here and there memorizing other peoples stories, trying to make them their own. Some of the greasy spoons in this town even require a headshot with your application.

It's midnight and he'd gotten out of there so fast his apron is probably still swinging on the hook where he'd thrown it. Here, at the corner of Sunset/Fairfax, sitting at the bus bench and cracking a 2/$3 bottle of RiteAid Shiraz, eyes closed, inhale, hold three seconds, exhale, sip, laugh. Laugh about the horror of it all. The searching. The demands for service. The way we all look tired. On the outside. On the inside. Hiding or accentuating the broken pieces.

Laugh at yourself, but also to yourself, he thinks. Lest you be the man laughing alone on a bus bench. And maybe those cats have the answer. Maybe thats what's so goddamn funny. What is he looking for? Where is he going, with this job? Seeing the lifers, those guys/gals who've been there 20, 25, 35 years, he knows that won't be him. So what now? What next? What is the purpose? If this is only a stop on a longer journey, why here? Why now? To what end?

Some customers never tip a cent. Brazenly cheap as they sign for $6,000 worth of wine soon to sit in a humidity controlled cellar till Paul is down to fingering his last nickel. Only to pop the bottles as he's lowered into the ground, blissfully unaware of his existence. He doesn't fault them for being rich. Just for being out of touch. Some are pricks, all emphasize their friendships with the owner, who often denies these claims.

There are as many problem rich people as there are poor. The money comes to some & not to others, fine. But how about all the dick sucking lip service we give to these rich philanthropists, your Bono's of the world? Music tastes aside, enough is enough. If you are privileged with time/or money, inherited or earned, it's your moral fucking duty to change the world for the better. It's like singing the praises of a parking attendant who keeps the lot from jamming up. Your just doing your job. What if he, Paul, got the presidential medal of freedom, the nobel peace prize, started trending on google, every time he gave a bum a buck and a smoke? Don't we have a moral imperative to stop exalting those who are only holding up their part of the bargain.

The windows are down on the way back from Bel-Air, where he'd lugged 25 cases of wine up and down and up again, every staircase of this splendidly modern, designed-to-look-old mansion, without so much as a thank you. Shadowed through the house by a droning twenty-something who couldn't say enough about his appreciation for the working man. No thanks for Paul specifically, but this guy wanted to marry and fuck the working man. Cornering him each time he was finally able to set down a case in the marble tiled, oak shelved, wine vault, (there were so many stairs, ups, downs, twists and turns, he couldn't even say if it was a cellar, under or above ground, or where in the house he even was at any given moment), to explain how he knew that Paul wasn't getting paid shit. He knew because his mother didn't pay the workers at the house enough to live on. Explaining that, once all of this was his; sure he got an allowance now, but once it was all his, he'd make a real change in the way things operated. Lugging and sweating, grunting occasionally, Paul watched the dull, chubby eyes of this heir apparent watching him work.

When he'd finished unloading the cases and caught his

breath, watching this man living in the reality of a child signing the receipt, he could almost feel sorry for him. Or at least sympathize. Paul knows what it is to feel impotent. To compensate or lay blame, to self aggrandize, in the face of helplessness. They'd moved across the grounds, and it took what seemed like minutes to traverse such a large space of land, toward the equally large, King Kong capacity entry gate. Without thinking, spouting some sarcastic comment like, Think you got enough gate there? Causing the man's face to brighten and fade quickly. You shoulda seen it before my mom made us take down the razor wire down.

Of course he'd gotten no tip. And he'd been out on this one delivery for nearly two hours, which means he's lost potential cash from other deliveries. But at least he's been out of the shop for two hours right? Trying to put a positive spin on things. Trying to...

He's driving east on Fountain when it happens. A hard whack on the right side of his head and some other chaos. Looking down at his hands holding the passenger side mirror. Where the hell did this come from? What the hell is going on here? People run towards the car. Shhiiiittttt. I'm fucked i'm fucked im fucked! Remembering that he's not had a drink today. Halloween. Hadn't had time to stop. The gods on his side. He still might be fucked though. A hangover-like throbbing suddenly accentuated. Lighting a cigarette and stepping out onto the square torn patch of grass below the car.

Some clean/hippie lookin' cat stands next to a Mercedes that's half buried in the front right quarter panel of the delivery van. They exchange info, each smoking their respective cigarette. Now the bystanders chip in with advice. You got to move these cars. Can't move 'em 'till the cops come. You guys all right? ...sit down deep breaths I saw the whole thing....neck injury....move the cars don't move the cars.... A motorcycle cop drives by without a glance.

It's only a few hours into his shift and he still has the whole night ahead, nerves crackling on edge, if he doesn't loose his job. Assuming he will. Getting the engine going is a plus and limping bent axle shaking violently & veering, he maneuvers the van back to the deli. Smell of burnt rubber and metal sharp in his nostrils. Now the fucker won't go left. So he circles the block with right turns twice before managing to get it into the parking lot. He'd assumed the car was insured. Hopes it is since, not having a car himself, he has none of his own. Isn't even sure if that's how insurance works.

Everyone has to figure out the thing, the way to look at life and see it for what it really is. To see the space of things and people, and how they occupy that space in relation to the other things and people. Nouns. Paul has to learn his own way of remembering how the nouns are precious. All the nouns in all their different ways. Any time spent not appreciating nouns is time spent not appreciating nouns. He wants to remember that, each thing seems better, in some way, in hindsight. If he can remember that so well that he just knows it, maybe it can help make things better in the moment. He's lost himself now. Not sure if that even makes sense.

But, point is, finding a way of looking at things. A way of going into looking at things. Like a still-life by Wolfgang Tillmans. The sweet raw yellow of a tomato resting atop a pile of newspaper. Trying to think of things like that. Finding and dissecting, knowing about something or not knowing, but seeing that it is. That nouns (and emotions and situations) are. Why is it easier to look at a picture, a film, and find the beauty? It must be that beauty is simple and always present, but constantly obstructed by immediacy or connection to self. Then, things must be looked at simply and beauty will be revealed?

He goes down to check the mail. Management has yet to put his name on the gold art deco mail cubby for room 615, so he did it himself. It has no bearing. Offering him more a sense of semi-permanence, than any practical value. Nothing but coupon packs and various card stock junk mail. Not that he's expecting anything. Any business not done online or in a shop seems like a scam now anyway. Christ, all the old mail order catalogs from the not too distant past. Those thick books of gloss or newsprint, with weirdly written product descriptions, and dimensions, price and payment options.

Shipping/Handling seemed like such a mysterious job to a young Paul. The cryptic world of logistics. Everything getting smaller as he's gotten older. He'd worked the shipping/handling rackets and there was very nothing much to 'em. But there were so many things that seemed like something while you were doing them. Tension in the workplace. How is that a thing we let into our lives? He can't be bothered by allowing work to fuck with his vibe. But he does and is. He's often religiously bothered at work. Every customer, red light, phone call, doorman, elevator, bad tip, missed turn, everything bothering. Until he notices it. It's a powerful moment to realize you've worked yourself up for nothing. Grown a little tumor in your body for a job that involves sandwiches or, much of anything else. He knows he needs to be, thinks anyway, the kind of guy who understands anything. Getting cut off (in traffic or conversation), shitty service in a restaurant, bad luck, good luck, etc. He wants always his first thought to be: This is something. It's ok.

To be rousted from the bus is a rare achievement, even for him. The mustachioed bus driver slapped his face & apologized, maybe. Or he'd just got off at the end of the line. On a street corner. Dark. Thinking difficult, walking more so. Somewhere there is home, although he can't picture where. Least of all in relation to his current whereabouts. Phone dead, no one to call anyway. Little control of arms and legs. A half boiled noodle pin-balling through the unknown.

Beer bellied whores & wiry crackheads sweep debris to piles along the sidewalks with their pacing. Attempting to ask directions, mouth full of glue, disconnected from any thought process. Each tripping step toward some liquor store. Carddeclinedcarddeclined-carddeclined. Spitting out enough words for a promise of compensation, he finds himself under the guidance of some scrawny street machine, tuned up & wide eyed on something.

At the bus stop, sprung up from nowhere mirage all around, the old junkie asks for his 20 spot. Paul swipes and re-swipes the card, every card, at a dirty ATM a stone's throw from the bus stop where the man sits statue still. Starring at the dead black screen of his phone. Sliding another card. If he'd promised the cat a twenty for safe passage he wants to deliver. The geezer'd done his part. In the end he unearths a crumpled dollar in his coat pocket. Handing it over. Mumbling from both parties. The moment when two shaking hands from two shaking bodies hold the same dollar and wonder why there isn't more.

This is a hospital. He seems to know before waking. Feels almost like a destiny. Like a plan. Rough scratching gown crunching blue around part of him. On the verge of pulling out the i.v. he thinks better of it. Hits the call button, then pulls the tube anyway, almost fainting, to watch the skin pull against the sucking passage of the needle. A round brown nurse appears. Tired genie of pills & potions. She's telling him he'd pissed himself. Was found on the steps of a church. He imagines them cold.

Throwing his legs over the side of the bed to right himself, almost passing out again but persevering. People die in hospitals. Wrong leg amputated, infected blood, illness thrives & mutates into the super-bug of tomorrow. Will he have to pay for this? Sign nothing. He hadn't wanted help. Hadn't asked for it had he? No, they tell him. Someone called 911. Why should he be responsible for some upright citizens concern?

They brought him here and now they won't let him leave. He has work in a few hours. Maybe. What day is it? When had he been brought in? How long? Has he missed work? What day is it? And what day had he been brought in? So it's been 5 hrs? They tell him to wait in bed for the doctor. Only a few minutes. Please?

Walking barefoot over the linoleum, the sticky peeling sound feeling like home. A shiver climbing back into the bed. After ages, he's up again. This time, the nurse elsewhere for the moment, leaving him free to wander.

Stepping through a doorway to a hall, occupied by a lone hospital bed and the lonely girl in it, he approaches curiously. Same blue paper suit. She asks for a magazine, her brown hair cropped close. Early 20's, thin pale arms, thin pale legs barely making mounds like wrapped straws below the static cling blanket. They talk, her holding the magazine open, absently. Both in for alcohol poison. Both new to LA. New-ish. Paul climbing into the bed, her making room by scooting, with his help, nearer to the wall. Flipping the pages of a tabloid rag, the fashion police, celebrity baby gossip, them laughing, pointing out the most compelling unnecessary information.

The round brown nurse is a bowl of jelly running down the hall, shooing him back to his own bed. Head shaking. Don't you know you smell like piss? He thinks she might laugh. After a once over from the doctor they begin the process of reintegrating him into society. His pants, shirt, etc. He's pleased to find out this is Cedars. As pleased as one can be about an unexpected hospital stay. The 14 bus & he'll be home. Listening to the nurse and doctor whisper while he buttons his jeans, peering through the curtained partition.

...but can we discharge him? With that much booze in him he shouldn't even be able to stand.

He's practiced at it. If he's up and around there's nothing much else we can do for him. The doctor replies but doesn't look up from his phone.

Gathering up his belongings, unbelievable that everything is as it should be. Wallet, keys, lighter, scraps of paper, broken tooth-pick. Inside the wallet he finds $sixty-three. Had it been there all along? Had he ever been out, following the scamp expedition leader, flailing through torn ghetto streets? Or had it all been some church front drooling dream? He'll never know. Like all post-blackout days, which is to say, most days, now begins the slow process of letting the information find its way back in. Too much direct searching of the mind revealing nothing. He must loosen the receptors and allow the fragments to arrange themselves. He would rather forget the implosion had ever happened but it is some psychological need he has to relive the horror and embarrassment, a need to know what he'd done and how he'd acted. Who he needs to apologize to, or avoid.

Outside the CVS at Beverly/La Cienega, he waits 45 min for the liquor hour when he buys 2 bottles of nitrate infused red. Bag of bottles in hand, cigarette drawing to a close, up trundles the bus. Things are already looking up. Sitting in the back of the bus, feeling the plastic hospital bracelet on his wrist, not dissimilar to a festival bracelet and the feeling, mind and body, after the long excesses of a festival weekend. Realizing with some shame, and some laughable irony, that he is the disheveled, unhealthy looking guy, tagged with the scarlet letter of addiction that he's so often seen boarding busses and wondered at.

Back in his room at the Dicksboro, he throws the discharge paperwork on the table and pops the cork on one of the bottles. Removing the filthy jeans & shirt, he throws them in the trash where they won't, for the moment, remind him of his excesses. Lay in bed a while, sipping the wine. It's the only thing to do. The only thing that can be done right now. Then, shower off the troubles of yesterday. Burn his skin cooked lobster red, scouring off the thick barnacles of dead cells, piss & dirt. Feeling new. The freshness of possibilities. Antidote for the chaos of days, weeks, nights events. Almost convincingly bolstering his spirits with the fiction that he is living a life worth commenting on. That these are his stories of youth and revolt. But his youth is waning, his revolt misguided. Something has to change. But not today. Can't today. Tomorrow. If there is a tomorrow, he will proceed from there. If not for him, someone else can take up the mantle.

He pushes himself up and out of bed, grabbing the discharge paperwork and scanning it before lying back down. .52% blood alcohol. Didn't know it could get that high. A certain pride rises from his survival, from knowing that death has touched him again, but could not get a firm hold. He's immediately put off by this reaction, knowing his tempting fate is childish. Acting out. Sad. On the last page a dark printed bold line: STOP DRINKING TO EXCESS! followed by info on local detox centers and substance abuse hotlines.

His phone is charged now and he's got a firm grasp on what day it is. Calling work, he tells them he's been in the hospital. Tells them he was mugged. They tell him to get someone to cover his shift and over the next three hours he calls the same three numbers three times each, sipping wine and leaving messages, sends the request, along with a brief explanation via text, fingers crossed, making promises of recompense.

No one else can ever really know the horror of it. Not that his is any exceptional experience, just that it is his alone, 24/7/365. Even he has the large black spots. He's missed the last two days of work in the first shaking, sweating, sleepless phase of detox. Alternating between worry and placid calm. The calm comes at the exact moment when the worry becomes too much, the mental & physical strain making him wonder if he's already got wet brain, if this dissociative fugue is permanent. Then, respite. He can close his eyes, the pins and needles still pinning and needling, but there is something like peace for a time. Back to worry. About the days he's missed, the money he's not making, the fact of the accident, the overwhelming sense that everyone knows he's been drunk, is drunk, will always be drunk. It is dramatic, alcoholism. It is death-defying, death-wielding, it is wicked and clean and pure, and hopeless, and so brimming over with truth in certain moments that to not break down and weep at the beauty is unthinkable, the breaking down as further proof of the hopeless ever-churning severe splendor of the void.

But that's just life. There's a million and one different scams to get hung up on, and, like as not, Paul'll be stuck on one of 'em at any given time, maybe more, and more after that, down on into perpetuity, and letting go of one weight doesn't help when your made of magnets. So no one will ever really know what his life has been. He'll never be able to recall all the questions he's asked himself, all the faces and things he's seen, all the blackout nights knowing nothing but the slow beckoning sense of death in the dark of still room alone, all the fuck it's yelled in response, take me now, to hovering inevitable specter filling all the space and time, inching itself into the bottoms, out of the tops of planted empties, behind the dry dusty spaces by the bookcase, tickling at the edges of the room that exists with the whole world inside it made of nothing, and the waiting for that death that seems to be right there. And then it's gone. And there's no one really to tell 'cause, try as he might, it's just not as grand to anyone else. They only see him as a minor character in their own story. So he can try to tell the people, who don't, can't, listen. But they get it. They get it just the same way he does. Cause he's not going through anything different than anyone else. There's nothing so groundbreaking about his Feature Presentation. Some interesting stories? Sure. But only really interesting in their synchronicity. In the way they parallel the shared struggles of the human experience. Interesting in the way the main character sees him/herself as the main character. That his feeble gasp of life, no matter how broad or majestic it can become, his vary existence, is and always will be unknown and meaningless and ridiculous to billions of other struggling humans.

Then we are united by our struggle. That seems like too grand a statement to be utterly true. But we are united by something. Maybe something as simple as proximity. If death is coming, closer at each breath, around every corner, from out of the ground or sky or on a pizza, if death is coming, as it surely is, how should he spend his time? In the pursuit of something, the application of something, the building or demolition or the practice of something? Is it safe to be a worker amongst workers, man amongst men? By safe he thinks he means is it giving up? To strive toward a certain uniqueness has always been his goal but, could there be, is there a way to take on the responsibilities of the world, of adulthood, without loosing yourself in the process? Is it enough to be pleasant, to devote yourself to the improvement of things in an immediate way, in your immediate space? If he could just find a way to get out of bed in the morning. His life seems proof enough that whatever he is doing hasn't been/isn't working. How do you know when you're walking the line if you can't see it? With the infinite number of lives he'll never lead, never knowing anything about so many things, unaware of the amount of things he can't even begin to imagine that are happening on and in his body right now. How many things are going on in this perfectly still room (the wood is a not solid jumble of intricately moving things he cannot see, or is it just a table?)?

He will have to make peace with the fear of missing out, abandon the idea that each choice is paramount, accept what is and what has been, staying hopeful and open to what can be. Are the time and anguish he spends thinking about the table at an atomic level, wondering about the particle structures, studying the movement of the molecules, is it all worth it, or is it just a table to put a sandwich on while you watch t.v.? It's probably all of these. Maybe he should stop thinking about things so much, but he won't, or maybe he will eventually, or… who knows.

He can't eat yet, but the puking and heaving have stopped for the moment. The sweat has drenched him through and he's glad to have clean clothes to change into before wrapping himself in a blanket and lighting a cigarette. Staring at the refracted glowing pearl of the embers reflection in the sunken face of a dull spoon. Moving his head with his hips, watching the pearl gliding starry shimmer across the surface. This is a moment in his life. The ridiculous moment of his distraction by semi-shiny object. It is fine. It is small. It is a singular and worthwhile experience, no better or worse than the summit of any peak or the glitz of any flash bulb paparazzi. This moment holds as much virtue as any. He will never get the time back from this cigarette. Will never get the future time back that this cigarette may be taking away. That is ok. The quality of life is not measured in how you spend it, or how long you spend it for, but the ability to deal with the idea that it is being spent. As anarchy is to believing in nothing, Paul wants to be to believing in everything.

Aware of a barely subconscious hope that one day he will be celebrated for having such a great thought.

It's been two weeks now. Fourteen days since his last drink. This is how he always feels in sobriety. Every time he's given it a go, like he could never go back to that other way, so surprised by how good everything is and how he could have let himself live in that dark space for so long. Full of possibilities, the world spread out before him, opening, revealing itself and offering everything, anything, he wants. Walking 3rd Street, the sun is brighter. The birds sing their zippy tunes more beautifully and he feels like he can understand, like he could whistle back in response so he does. Each face looks happy or hopeful, as if his well being has overflowed, permeating, gladdening the hearts of the populous. Every city moment nearly overwhelms his senses, practically buckling his knees with it's timeless purity. We are one. All of us and every thing. The stone structures throw out their shelter of shade in greeting, trees exhale clean and fresh to sustain our inhalations, cats fuck & cry in alleys, the ice cream man smiles toothless and his carts wobble massages the bell to jingle in time with a christian hymn that stumbles from a radio. Things grow, things die, their beauty transcends joy or sorrow or fear or loneliness. Now is all we have and it is enough.

He shares twenty minutes and a few cigarettes with a hobo at the corner of 3rd and La Brea. Listening to the man. Really listening and responding and not overthinking compassion. Letting it flow around them. To brighten a day as his have been seems, more than ever, a duty and a thing that's worth what it's worth just because it is. The man cries. Laughs at his crying. Cries more. I just feel like scum. I know I stink, I can see the looks people give me when I get on the bus, he tells Paul. The way they pull their shirts up over their noses. I'm 64 years old, man. I won't lie, I'm an alchy. I had a job as a construction worker till 3 years ago. I've been out on the street since then. I don't want to be filthy, man, but I can't get no clothes. 40 yrs. of work and now I can't get any clean clothes. I'm sorry man. It just hurts. And you seem to understand. Right over there, he points to Beverly Hills, everyone's got so much goddamn money and their big ass houses and fancy cars and they won't even look at you. Don't treat you like a human. Like your a piece of shit to step over. I'm sorry man.

Isn't there a place, a shelter or the goodwill or something where they pass out clothes, Paul asks.

They don't really give out clothes too often, and when they do, guys usually fight their way to the font and grab everything they can. There's people down there on skid row who'll pull up with a hundred pizzas, or Carl's Jr. and stuff like that but, I'm headed downtown right now for a shower, costs 25¢, but after that I'll be wet and have to pull on these filthy fuckin' clothes again. In six months I get my social security. I only gotta make it six more months man, but I'm worried I won't. It's fuckin' hard out here man. It's hard and cold or hard and hot, but the safety of home, the comfort of being able to be indoors or out when you WANT to, man, you can go crazy without that. If I can make it six months, when I start to get that money, I'm gonna really try to get sober by then, so's I can get an apartment, one of those Section 8 places downtown, I'll be getting $600 a month and, god, that seems like a fortune to me now.

Paul hands the guy a couple'a bucks when the bus pulls up and watches his obscured shape move to the back and find a seat, waving through the window as they pull away. It doesn't make him sad. He's hopeful. The guy has a plan. Is trying to get sober. Paul knows that feeling and tries to send out some kind of vibe, some positive ions to help a ragged soul through that six months, through the rest of his life.

Walking to the Farmer's Market on Fairfax he enters the canopied open air food court and orders an omelet and coffee from Charlie's. Finding and sitting at a table, drinking the coffee amongst the milling bodies, a breeze cooled by the shadows funnels through past the fruit vendors and the nut hut and the Mongolian BBQ joint, blowing back the hair of everyone in that continuously long line before swirling the steam from his coffee and moving on.

His order's called. Denver omelet and white toast with blackberry jam eaten. Picking the little berries from his teeth as he moves to a smoking area and lights a cigarette for desert. He is full of self control, self awareness, compassion. The sun shines down and warms his bones and those of everyone in Los Angeles. It's beautiful. Life is a thing to marvel at. A cold beer would take the edge off the heat. Knowing he is an alcoholic will keep him from having more than one or two, so he passes back into the shade and pulls up at a bar stool next to Charlie's and orders a drink. Everything moves through him. The cold sweat of the glass is soft and dreamy.

Gently placing the wine bottle atop the thin tile ledge of the shower in a balancing act that keeps it out from under the water but close at hand. Brace for the crash. 1 2 3 4 . whew. He could place it on the sink but has tried that. All the reaching out and in getting water everywhere The water burning his pores, slipping off hair and nose in weak streams. Drink from the bottle. The cheap wine with its puckered lips leaving his mouth dry, tasting and feeling like soggy toothpicks. Lather with a scented gel compound from a plastic bottle. Reminded by his routine of a Patrick Bateman mantra. Laughing with the breeze that enters through the swollen wood frame of the shower window, tickling, drying the parts of his body not directly under the water. The skin feels tight, clean shrunken leather on the zephyr. Drink from the bottle.

He'll board the 4 bus to echo park; board the redline first, up Vermont to the hospital where at night the empty doorways and alcoves become clotted with men and women who fight the cold/hot/hunger/self with pipes and pills and shouts, flashing fists and bottles, whose curdling blankets weep from their sunken shoulders over sagging chests. She'll be at Taix, which was her call, this girl Rebecca who he met online. Taix with its heavy sumptuous bar & the fireplace that slowly stains the dark leather of the cushions and employees. Online dating is a thing now. People prowling through thousands of algorithmically suited profiles looking for love or a quick piece of ass. Paul knows people who've found both but he's still vaguely against it. Against the inorganic vibes, the implications, the lack of story involved in the meeting process. But at this point, fuck it, he thinks. What's one way vs another? Maybe in this case it's the destination not the journey.

Paul exits the blinking eye of the bus and buys a single sunflower from the standalone shop with the white swooping roof. The winos huddle in clumps, shadows stretching long in the sunset, passing cigarettes and pleasantries there since sunrise when they left the shelter beds and clinics.

Rebecca is 27 according to the internet. Her long black hair sporting a peroxide blond stripe in front, pinned and sprayed into a curlycue pompadour type job. In her profile picture her hairline is punctuated with a dark reptilian rose. She has, or applies, rosy cheeks with high cheek bones on either side of a cute upturned nose, pierced through the left nostril. Cat-wing lashes hovering voluptuous over dark Latin eyes. A lawyer for some production company involved in reality tv. She works long hours trying to figure how to keep shows with unstable housewives, pregnant teens or racist homophobes, screaming pageant mothers or kitten hoarding duplex dwellers on at primetime. Trying to appease sponsors who hock dick pills made from the blood of endangered pinatas and pizzas with candy coated crusts.

They've spoken for a total of about 3 hrs. over the phone and sent texts back and forth for a week, Paul unsure of the sexting etiquette, knowing that's how the kids are doing things these days but feeling, as a person who dislikes texting in general, like…well, like a fucking tool. But he also doesn't want to seem like a goody two-shoes. He wonders if this isn't a mistake, bringing all this technology into relationship interactions, especially at the beginning. But these are the times we live in. Until there's an electronic infrastructure collapse, which he is hoping for, things will probably only keep heading in the direction of quantity over quality. More distant, less personal communication. Sometimes he feels the urge to be incommunicado after leaving the house.

Once, they had even face timed. Looking at the small screen in his hand, thinking about that scene in Demolition Man with the chick in the shower and her naked video misdial to Stallone. Returning his attention to Rebecca, they spoke in low tones and he watched her breasts heave sway stutter beneath her snug clothes with each breath and laugh. She had a crooked recessed tooth which supplied her with a precocious quality that at once took him off guard and filled him with lust. Desire to see her undress, to undress her, to see her walk down the street or sitting on the long ledge of an open window, somewhere in a brick walled loft Downtown with her legs crossed under her, toes wiggling absently as a ray of sun illuminated the dust hanging from the air around her.

The shower wine warms his gut, boils there, pleading for companionship as he sinks into the wooden chair closest to the fire. He orders whiskey. Pupils dilate to black saucers in the tavern warm glow. His hand is remembering the sunflower it clutches and is now leaving it to wait at a small side table with a mosaic top. The booze is delivered in a tall slim glass full of ice. He'll ask them to forgo the ice next round. Hoping for more bang per buck.

The whiskey quiets his mind and, along with the fire, he feels a small warm quiver reach for his spine as the comfort of that familiar blanket descends, slowing his heart, a hazy dull cloud erasing life's rigid infrastructure, leaving the muscles relaxed and tuned. Wandered deeper into the soft tunnels of his mind, forgetting why he's here.

She's beside him now. Taking off her leather jacket and ordering a drink. Apologizing for being late. He'd been brought back by a change of smell. A think velvety rope of vanilla that pulled him from the wide empty cellar of his thoughts. She sits. The fire dancing naked shadows across her face. A few stray hairs on her head glowing. Phosphorescent larva floating through moonlit ocean currents. She is talking about her father, about being raised in LA, about living in New Mexico. She smiles, raising her vodka tonic, exposing the recessed tooth.

So what do you do? Art-wise I mean, she asks. Well, he doesn't know how else to say it, nothing really. Or, this and that; drawing, writing, painting, photography. I spend a lot of time thinking I guess. About why these things are worth doing. If they're worth doing for me, if I'm any good at any of them, and, if I had enough money, whether I would still want to do them. If they can even be done, when everyone has already done everything worth and not-worth doing. I don't know if it's only because, I mean, if I'm already struggling, and if feels like I am— I know I'm not on a global scale, or even a local scale really— but if I'm already struggling, shouldn't it be towards something that I've found meaning in, like art? Shouldn't I try to pass on those little glimpses of freedom that have been afforded to me?

An expression has settled on her features but, knowing her little as he does, it's hard to tell what emotion to read there. This look has the characteristics of smugness but he tries to believe it's interest. That she had expected a simpler answer is obvious. Does she think he's just another one of the thousands in Hollywood who sell themselves as the idea of an artist? Another upstart who's just in it for the image, the buffoonery that such a title allows? Maybe he is. Does she consider such an enterprise, even when pursued sincerely, to be a lesser calling unless there is real money being made?

Swirl the round hollow ice cubes with the red cocktail straw. Watch the peroxide blond stream of hair drain clockwise down her dark features. He remembers the flower. Handing it to her, it seems loud, impossibly large and bright in the clandestine earth tones of the bar. What? she asks. The Echo. We could check out the Echo. See what there is to see, he repeats. The waitress leans through, over their shoulders, trying not to spill the fresh round of drinks. He thinks Rachel is buzzed. Maybe she won't notice he's a drunk. I know the bar tender. He's a creep, but we can swing some free drinks. she offers. Paul turns on a smile and a nod, wondering but not really caring about her relationship with this bar tender.

He would rather stay by the fire. By the fire, floating in his whiskey blanket, watching her. Picking a few petals, the widest and thickest from the edges of the flower, she leans close enough to drop them in. Watch them burn and turn to dust. He studies the curve, from her cheek bone down her neck. One liquid smooth silhouette line encasing her flesh, peaked dew drop breast hanging in profile, gliding down and into the waist, tapering out again to form the robust ass. He pictures a creepy bar tender. Tries to picture a not creepy one. Finding this more difficult.

Rachel had spent the last 4 hours arguing with some jackass from Dallas. She has to argue a lot at work. It's pretty much her whole job, she says. She wouldn't want to argue with him, he thinks. This could be good. You ready? She's risen from her reverie above the fire and is again armoring herself in black leather. As I'll ever be, from Paul, who holds the shouting flower at his side. What if she's conditioned by work and nature, years of school and study to communicate solely through argument. This could be bad.

Stepping out into the night, the low gel buzz filled neon suffocating the sidewalks, echoing on glassy window panes; it seems brighter at night -frantic- Slip an arm around her waist on the blvd. She shoots a look, his hand presses the warm firm pillows of her hip bones. He is caught in her eyes, being swallowed by waves of droning light, drifting lazily on a stream of white noise— dragging his hand through wet electric waters. His voice comes back with an answer, a question. Strumming her spine. Wondering at what little skin and pulp lays between the touch of their bones.

Oh god I want tacos. She pulls him toward a taco truck. Do you want tacos? Yeah I want tacos. Who doesn't want tacos, Paul answers, humming Streams of Whiskey. He pictures ducks diving, their eyes bloodshot and slick. TACOS AL PASTOR ASADA POLLO LENGUA TACOS AL PASTOR ASA…. primary color LED lights scroll past on loop. In the big rock candy mtn. you never change your socks… There's always a long line… or none. He agrees.

Standing in the crowded wafting clouds of grease he sees and feels and seems, far away. Disconnected in close proximity. Ride the swelling moment. He will let all of humanity in, just for a moment. Will let all his molecules fly and mingle and feast on the microcosm street corner scene and return to interpret the moment for him. He waits. Near a tipping point. Nothing. Maybe something? This is something.

She pays for the tacos. As they eat she wonders about him. He had told her he was an artist. She thought he had, that first time she'd face timed him, late night after a few drinks and a little blow with the girls, when she'd gotten home, feeling alone, postpartum after-party. Now he tells her he's a delivery driver. Or, that that's how he pays the bills, for now. That none of the things he does define him. She's a little disappointed, or confused, but tries not to let it show. She's suspect that he's just another aimless layabout. An avoider of reality. Wondering if he's the same type of hard drinking no account as her last boyfriend. It doesn't matter really. She can see him again, or not. Their conversations up to this point had shown similar interests and some amount of comfortability, only a little awkwardness.

He seems disjointed now. She knows that he's drunk but it seems like something else. He looks lost and tired. He's been listening, responsive and animated but she couldn't… I mean, he's acting nice enough. A vague smile. She wants someone kind. She always says so. No, someone genuine, in anger or joy. But also, nice. Why is it so hard to find someone who's nice and doesn't need looking after? Will he try to fuck her tonight? If he does, she will take it as a compliment but make sure it remains at try. Save all that for later. She answers his questions and poses her own between bites, the little glossy pools of red/orange grease splotching their white paper plates, turning them waxy clear.

Discarding her last half taco, more grease than tortilla at this point, she studies the lines of his face. Disengaging the features to take them in as individual entities. The triangular aquiline nose—he looked at the birdlike mr. brooks—the rigid brow line. The future potential of a receding hair line. She doesn't put him at more than 30 but he seems childlike. Peculiarly intriguing.

This is my building. I just need to go up to shower and change. Then we can head out. They walk up the wooden stairs, scarred and worn slick. Her body sharpens for the impending creak, hoping he isn't looking at her ass, knowing that, if he is, these pants make it look good. Hoping this isn't something she'll regret. Hoping she'd remembered to save and email the finalized contracts for Monday.

Paul sits on the couch rubbing his hands over the red velvet fabric, across the worn spots— a mangy dog of a couch. The 3rd floor studio is much like his own. An original painting by Sylvia Ji hangs above the bureau. There is the pervasive aura of a defunct brothel, without the musty smell that one might expect. The room has some of the hallmarks of every twenty-something's pad he's ever been in, but there is something simultaneously found and store bought. The place fits into itself.

In the kitchen he pours wine into two well worn plastic Dodgers cups and takes a discreet pull from the bottle of vodka on the round cafe style table. A hundred sunken eyes stare at him from the grinning bone of embroidered sugar skull tablecloth. Replace the bottle, smoothing the wrinkles from their faces and his own.

How does she see him? What notions are already impressed upon her mental image of his whole. We make guesses or assumptions about the parts of people we don't yet know informed by the bits we do. He is doing so with her. She's comfortable bringing a strange drunk man up to her apartment on a first date. How many men had sat here? How recently? How many had she fucked on the big 4 post bed with its rumpled black sheets? Tabling his drink and laying face down, he inhales. Exhale hot breath deep into her pillow. Inhale the whiskey/vodka/wine/sleep/perfume of his breath mingled with her skin cell hair follicle scent. Flipping to his back he makes angels of the sheets. A rumpled silk vitruvian man. Her fat black cat jumps on the bed to lay on his stomach, nuzzling its head in the crook of his neck.

She likes you, Rachel says, coming out of the bathroom, but then again she likes everyone. Wet hair seeping circles on the shoulders of a fresh shirt. Paul is laying on her unmade bed. She feels embarrassed at the mess, then a hint of anger that he's been so presumptuous as to make himself at home. She had told him to do so, but people don't usually get comfy so quick. He's handing her a cup of wine and gives a toast. To lives too short, and days to long. They tick the plastic cups together. Drink the wine. her face in the wine, its reflection looking past her. Looking around the room, trying to see it how he might be seeing it. How he might be seeing her. She suddenly feels awkward in her own rooms, in her skin. What should she be doing with her arms, glad to have the glass to occupy a hand. Watching him watch her light a cigarette and follow suit.

...I did some work with her husband and he sent it to me from Nigeria as a thank you. They are talking about a small sculpture on the nightstand; angular male frame drenched in shadow, groovin' high on a reed flute as djinns circle the edges of darkness.

Back at her apartment, post show, their hands explore what bodies feel like. After making out, swaying softly, feeling alone to-gether in the dense crowd under the disco ball spin. After drinking the wine. After the whiskey and the cigarettes and the wine. Going at it, he can't believe he's got it up, is keeping it up. She'd consent-ed with a smile (he thinks it was a smile), if that's what you want... Which now, midstream, seems awkward. Maybe she didn't really want this.

She was in charge, on top, signs pointing to enjoying herself, when the condom broke. Paul did not know this, and in hindsight, things had become more intensely enjoyable at some point. Neither did they know this when he came inside of her. They did know once he pulled out. Paul doesn't feel good about this turn of events. Ra-chel is not reacting well. Rightfully. But currently he can't breath to explain his feelings, or to agree with hers. He can only lay back and take the anger while he catches his breath.

... I'll have to spend $50 on the pill... He feels bad. Offers to pay for it—breath finally caught. It's not about the money. It's the time to go there, outta my day. It just sucks. Heart rate slowing. This was not the mood he'd hoped to achieve. He tries to be helpful with quiet empathy, not knowing if this is the right approach, till they fall asleep.

The next morning he watches her prep for work. Watches her reflection in the bulb-rimmed enclave of her vanity. Applying the lipstick, powders and perfumes. Stealing away to the kitchen at intervals to suck calm and courage from the bottle of vodka, chasing with glasses of water. He feels dirty. Whole. Good and empty. And when she's ready, pat-checking his pockets as they head out the door. Down the long corridor with the wooden planks of a ship's deck stretching away from them, knocking back at the bottoms of her boots, squeaking loosely beneath his converse. Down two flights of stairs and SLAM!, out into the curtain-less bright bedroom of Hollywood.

They are standing close when she kisses him. It's surprising, a better goodbye than expected, but his gaze remains elsewhere. On the sun colored streets, the little groups gathering and feeding and moving about in colonies and hierarchies, at the way this moment seems so intimately unrealistic, or, like they're both attempting to be the realized idea of people who aren't them.

At Sunset and Alvarado, waiting for a bus that will come eventually. He feels triumphant. Bold and reassured. A part of history, future, now. The fire of lusty decadent living born from the heaving streets of Los Angeles clings to his being, symbiotic. Allow for the emptiness that comes with it. Consume the landscape through the drag of a cigarette. She is driving away in her small newish car while he stands, head buzzing, taking off his jacket to feel the cold morning wind licking at the new sun that presses his flesh. Rubbing his face and running fingers through greasy hair, stretching out, trying to wring the hangover, the cold, the awkward night, from his every pore.

The world on his side, he pops into Happy Tom's for a coffee. Exit, coffee steaming, burning his hand on overflow as he tries to wave down and disrupt the quiet gliding past of the bus. His eyes meet those of the driver and he thinks he saw a smile as the orange vessel shifts gears, speeding past.

Woman and I walk through a wooded trail pulling those suitcases with the handles and the small plastic wheels bouncing unpredictably over dirt and small pebbles on the well worn path. There are overtones of hostility, sad bent bodies milling about. Small groups lay around with heads propped on duffel bags, hair and hooded sweatshirts or Gilligan caps shading their eyes from the lack of sun. A towering man with weighted cheeks that stretch the center of his face, walks past. "You ever been here before" he says more than asks without stopping. I follow with my eyes as he canters off. Woman is holding my hand, humming a tune I have never heard, reminding me of a child in a horror film. Sharp pain as the small branch of a nearby tree penetrates my arm just above the inside elbow and I look down to see creatures the size of bb's scuttle out under my skin. Heavy nausea grips me as I jerk away from Woman knowing that if I can pop the life out of these creatures, like little berries or peas, I might stand a chance. Their quick creeping along the inside of my skin lifting it away from the flesh as they scamper around. Picturing them tunneling as robotic spiders. And pop them I do. Having managed to remove the stick, which I presume to be their facilitator, before more than seven or 8 have entered. Popping them all, even with their efficient scattering, I turn to ask Woman if we should find a hospital. But Woman is gone, and I am left with two bags to roll. Raised bumps turning a slow purple remain visible on the parts of skin covering their exploded corpses. I picture the insides of the ladybug I popped as a kid, all greeny-orange and candy. Grabbing the warm handles of the suitcases and turning back to the road...

He wakes on the beach and lights a cigarette. Clouds have rolled in and the sea become the darker colors of the forest. The wind stabs at his fingers, nose, ears, all patches of exposed flesh as he smokes. Standing up and trying to keep as much sand out of his ass crack as possible, he plods, stepping forward, sliding back, through the sand towards the bus station.

A dinner at Miceli's for his one real work friend. Other, ancillary, friends will be there. Other co-workers. People he doesn't know. Only a handful of times in his life has he ever been invited to attend such an event. This is almost a dinner party. Well technically it is. I'm at a dinner party, he thinks. It's better and worse than I thought it would be. Standing inside the entrance, under the low light of casual sexual nostalgia, jacket draped over shoulder in his best McQueen impression. He's early, or unfashionably on time. Scanning a room full of shadowed and well lit faces, none of them familiar. For this friend's bday party he has brought many things, things that fit into pockets, but no wrapped gift. We are grown people, at least on the exterior, he reasons. There are two joints in a pack of smokes waiting to be realized, a pint of whiskey pining for a tryst with multiple lovers, slowly warming in a back pocket. Foreplay. So he wanders off down the blvd. Leaving the whiskey untouched for to share with the bday boy, ducking in and out of bars, pre-gaming.

Showing up for round two, now late for sure, fairly drunk and, once seated and surrounded by faces unfamiliar in their outside of work makeups and coiffures and formal attire, confused. Underdressed. Overly boisterous. This now feels like a family function where he is looked at with questioning eyes, a prowling creature, caged and truculent, better viewed from afar. He offers an under the table pour to the bday boy and gets a polite decline. Suggesting the joints then. They can go outside to partake. No one will notice. Polite decline. So Paul gets more drunk, openly swigging from the bottle and trying to make conversation with these hesitant, delicate, well mannered apparitions.

By the time of his second coming, everyone has already eaten. There is a couple on his left chatting about their dog to anyone who will listen. They are well dressed, well groomed, but unavoidably shlubby. At the piano someone plays a good rendition of Cannonball Adderly's *Work Song*. Paul growls a loud Yeah! of approval at the opening bars as polite conversation stops and all eyes turn to him. One of the fresh glowing faces at the long table is laughing at him. He laughs at himself, them, this situation. The piano man gives a nod of the head and Paul makes a mental note to ask if he knows any Zevon. These fuckers don't appreciate a good recital when they see one.

All the conversational tactics he has tried have born no fruit. Everyone has written him off. Although it doesn't seem like it to him, he knows he's probably got a pretty good slur going at this point, so he forgives them to himself, drifting into what probably seems like truculence, from the outside. You seem to be having a pretty good day. I didn't know it was your birthday too. Passive-aggressive comment from a distant corner of the table. No you're mistaken. I have no birthday. I am timeless. I am creation and destruction. I am the mirror of life and death, Paul replies shrugging. At least, this is what he thinks he has said.

Excusing himself and making a crawling under the table exit to the tune of many complaints, he heads for an alley to smoke one of the joints. Swimming in the last pull from the bottle, dragging deep a cigarette, a few, losing track of time, grabbing another bottle from a liquor store and downing it in one go. Walking, or something like it, back into the reception he sees a golden confetti laced party in the ballroom or foyer of a late 70's era hotel. Arms out to his sides he spins through a crowd of happy costumed men and women.

Yes I am mother natures son. Ooo Ooo. And I'm the only one. Lou Reed bangs off the walls and his brain.I do what I want and I want what I see. Paul yells back. Could only happen to me.

Magnetic metallic glitter exploding from the ceiling, whirling around the room sticking static to tits and elbows and ankles. People shine like articulated disco balls and Paul sees in a thousand mirrors his smiling face beamed back from each body he bumps into.

He passes out after creating this disturbance.

A frozen fish under my pillow. Its sweating, thawing eyes stare. Booze flowering out of the dead dilated pupils. I am horrified, picking up the fish, putting lips to one cold eye and drinking deeply.

His joints are the consistency of milk soaked cereal. Muscles ache and freeze in an aborted attempt at sitting up. Eyelids are caked shut with the hardened salivations of sleep and he pulls the crunchy crust off in gobs before exerting all the combined existing effort of the world in opening his face blinds. Feet and legs remain asleep, draped over the arm of the love seat he passed out on in Arnie's living room. Afraid that if he doesn't get the circulation going again soon he will lose the gift of mobility forever. Rolling off the couch to the hard floor, !Thwomp! Laying in the space between the sofa and the coffee table just wide enough for a body, he waits, comfortable in the closeness of the space, as the numb goes to tingle goes to harder tingle and finally toward normal.

Arnie is a 40-something tattoo artist who works from home. He is willing to do typical flash or lettering but lives for sci-fi themes. The apartment is usually a breeding ground of loose papers covered in drawings of spacey devilish beings and their transportation, sexy buxom alien women with ray-guns, books from Vonnegut and Jules Verne and Steve Perry. Paul met Arnie at a bar when the later asked for a cigarette. They began talking about tattoos and, after a few drinks, discovered they lived in the same building.

Arnie's got a woman. Or the woman's got Arnie. Or they both have each other. She told Paul they met while living in Manhattan's Lower East Side in the 80's. This previous residence alone is enough to raise a sort of idolatry in him. That locale being the scene of countless songs and stories he loves. Her name is Atike Beltran and she is a psychic. She has a theory that Jules Verne was a psychic. Arnie says that they met as kids while he and his friends were hanging in the basement of his apartment building smoking weed. According to him she wandered in, stared at them, hiked up her skirt, and began a standing urination, the only sound that of the stream of pee hitting the floor, never breaking eye contact, replacing the skirt and walking away.

She was 13 at the time, Arnie was 10. Later that night he ran into her in the hallway. Taking his hand and placing it upon her face, she told him the exact moment of his death. That was 30odd years ago and they've been together ever since. We live within the walls of a low decibel symbiotic gel pod, Arnie tells paul. Our spirits twine together through shimmering timelessness bound by ancestors in the past present and future, Atike says.

She walks around the house indolently. Always looking good in different pairs of the same tight, high-waisted pants and white blouse that hug her ripe curves. Always spotless, like the apartment, minus the loose papers. You can hear the click of her heels on the floor over the buzz of the tattoo gun as she brings Arnie a cup of coffee or more paper towels or just wanders around looking out windows.

This morning they're both still asleep. He's glad not to face them. Hopes they see him only as a character. Unreal, and by that virtue, impossible to be angry with. He hopes Atike can see his inner struggle. Hopes she can read his mind so as to understand, to not take offense or despise his intrusions. Hopes she can sense a lack of malevolence. Hopes there is a lack of malevolence to sense.

Now that he's got his legs back he looks around for any belongings, patented pocket pat check, and out the door. In the hallway he calls work, heart stalled in anticipation of a voice that knows, that was there last night, a voice that will say something to make him feel more awkward, more base and inhuman, to solidify his resolve to never show his face again. But the voice only tells him he has the next three days off. So he dings good morning over the threshold at Saver Liquor, dongs goodbye as he leaves, him and a bottle headed back to the cool stagnant comfort of the apartment above the world. To do his drinking 'till he feels his feet once again planted in the wholeness of dissolving.

Such an addiction to ritual. To things that make him feel better and the ones that make him feel worse. Wondering whether, subconsciously even, all his vices, even his positive and negative traits, are rooted in an need to practice repetition. It seems obvious. Just another way of saying comfort, contentedness, choosing the known, the familiar, over the untested. When drinking, putting on some Pogues, Muddy Waters, Hank Williams, music that sounds like drinking, that references drinking, deify's drinking, so engaged in the action, praying and sacrificing and chanting moving mantra of the thing, finding a near monastic piety in those movements. Or smoking- after a meal, before a meal, while taking a shit or drinking coffee, a thing to worship, to help engage conversation in public, something to do with his hands, distracting his mind for, never long enough, but as long as he can milk it.

Constantly shifting jobs, apartments, women, friends, fortunately or unfortunately bound to searching. Without having ever been aware of it until now. And, as always, unsure whether this is an answer, a partial answer at least, a clue, or just another fleeting delirium. Is he now, has he been for years, locked into the same ritualistic patterns, a sort of aborted phoenix? Self mutilation, the fire, ashes, a new beginning, faltering, ashes. Across all facets of his life he sees similar patterns, splotches of scorched earth.

In those rare moments of clarity between swigs, or on days of sobriety, he can see he's fighting the wrong battle. Or at least fighting the right battle the wrong way. He's fighting. Always having been told, through the rhetoric of countless centuries, that to win, to survive and thrive, one must fight. Fight against everything thats wrong, fight for everything that's right, fight for acceptance, relevance, equality justice success, against stress, depression, fear dilution evil misfortune addiction poverty ego...

Paul was once the age when a man would go to war, or more precisely, an age when a boy would be called to fight and listen without question. And there was a war on, at that time, and Paul was the right age for this war. He was a boy, and boys are sent to wars. But the draft had been out of fashion for some time by then, and he was lucky enough to have been born in a country that doesn't currently mandate military service. So he did not go to Iraq, to Afghanistan, and he fought a different battle at home, with himself and everyone around him. But he knew people, other boys and girls, who went and died, were mangled physically and mentally, who came home to a lukewarm reception at best. And what did they - our soldiers, the *enemy*, the people of those countries who were promised many things, the people here, in the US, who paid for all the boys and girls to die, all the machines to make war and ravage landscapes both natural and human - what did they get for all this fighting? It seems to Paul the answer is nothing. We, humanity, get nothing for the fight. We never have. Leastways nothing good.

What to do then when faced with the Hitler's, the Pol Pot's, the Bashar Al-Assad's, Ourselves? It is easy for Paul to think of justifications against military service, i.e. if everyone refused to fight there would be no fighting, how can I kill a man from another side who might be just as unwilling, just as frightened, just as lost or manipulated or acting out of a sense of duty as I am, etc. But it's unrealistic to think that abstinence from a fight is enough to prevent it, like so many other things, it works on paper but not in practice.

So, what then, is the answer? Paul had once known a man who told him, in reference to his time as a 17 year old marine during the tail end of the Vietnam War (which was over before he got there), The good Lord never gave me the opportunity to kill a man in battle. So Paul wonders if this is the answer. Not what was said, but the rooting out of this type of thinking, to keep young minds fresh, expose them to culture, explain the difference between assholes and people. Explain that there are hundreds, if not thousands, of different cultures, creeds, races, ideologies, religions, that none of them are wrong or right, but in every group there are assholes. It's our job, to attempt, through time and experience, to create less assholes as the years pass. To find new ways, empathic and just and passive ways of breaking down barriers, to develop, or at least embrace, new maxims and institutions for inclusive living, increasingly important in an expanding global consciousness. A more conscientious existence. If we are to claim superiority above other creatures, we should demonstrate our ability to act with control over our baser instincts, open up to love and life and all the other hippie/nouveaux-spiritual stuff (not even new, it's the same business all those philosophers and spiritualists have be *preaching*, mostly without *action*, for centuries). Of course there will always be wars, it's the imperfect nature of things, the snake and the apple, and who of us is not tempted by immediate gains?

And maybe this is yet another part of what Paul has been searching for, a conscientious inclusion, a putting in of work at the early stages, rather than waiting for the pinnacle, the tipping point, the conclusion, before action. There are several definitions of passive in the dictionary, Paul leafing through words sitting in his chair. Absently fingering the black indentations of each letter running down, diagonally, the fore edge of the pages. The one he thinks best describes his feelings about how to, ideally, live in the world is:

The main definition:

Accepting or allowing what happens or what others do, without active response or resistance.

And its secondary point:

Relating to or denoting heating systems that make use of incident sunlight as an energy source.

The problem with the former, as he sees it, there is no mention of utilizing the stimuli. Paul wants to inherit the incident sunlight, the little bright spots in each day, as an energy source. Also trying to keep in mind, before mounting stresses, before the inevitable grind of repetition sets in, that shadows exist because of light. He can use the slow healthy warm glow to propel him through the darkness. Or help fortify him in the realization that the darkness isn't bad, but temporary and different. Not to be a feared monster under the bed of a child's night, but a time for rest, rebuilding, letting go.

Life will continue in its oscillation between frantic hopeless groping and serene contentedness. And general sloth. And manic productions. He will have to accept these truths.

Fact: All the drinking has led him here and he must have learned something. But now he suspects that many of the learned things have turned out to be bad habits. Bullshits. Psychological limitations. Things manifest, even as subconscious physical extremes he notices in moments. Hunched, tense shoulders and shallow breathing of a wounded animal. Clenched eyes and teeth, thinking he's relaxed while laying in bed.

Life must be lived in the moment. But in the moment it is easy to lose perspective. To fall prey to old habits. The cunning of his devils. So he will continue reminding himself of his refusal to become one of the raging hollow scarecrows— the bitter, who leak constant criticisms and beratements. Who dole out gossip, nibble at hatred. He will be open, empathic, understanding, all the positive self talk bullshit that is right, whether or not he has spent his life hating it. And why not let go of cataloging what is socially good or bad? Why not just embrace those things that help, that make him feel whole? Because he is afraid. Are these the first fatal steps? Steps on a path toward khaki shorts and neon crocs, all that positive affirmation cheeseball self-help nonsense he's always despised.

What if those whimsical preachers are happy? What if, by continuing down a path of open acceptance, he becomes one of these homogenized mystic dudes he's worked to be so different from? Does he want happiness if it leads to that? All this, getting this far, only to wind up the thing he'd rallied against, fought as antithesis for so long?

Even now, are there some psychological inner workings at play of which he is unaware. The ever present temptations of compulsive over analysis. You are living in an overcomplicated manifestation of the world. Every question offering more questions with fewer and increasingly vague answers. And where is it getting you? He thinks this is something a therapist might say to him. He daydreams about going to a therapist. Someone who will say to him: Man you're fucked up. No wonder you're having such a rough time. But at every point of each day, he will remind himself it doesn't matter. None of it and all of it. Every breath a miracle. Every miracle impossible to appreciate above the trivial. And every trivial thing backed by an army of replacements.

So it's a choice. None of this, never accept defeat nonsense. To accept defeat is honorable and will always remain an option. An ending, broken and alone, seems the most likely scenario, given all the trials we're faced with. But, in defeat, the continuous spew of tribulations doesn't seem to lessen. No amount of drink or sobriety will save Paul from these difficult situations, pre-programed and unavoidable. No amount of fight or flight. No go with the flow. Only evolution, change, sustained searching toward some answerless question, continued pursuit of perspectively meaningless goals, deviations, the rabid cycle of tragic comedy that beats on, winless, lossless, in its inexplicable experimental way. Every cliche is true. Nothing is avoidable. He will hold his head up when he can. Dark seas will appear, the clouds will break open to reveal the sun, people will shit and die and fuck and satellites will orbit the earth for thousands of years at incredible speeds in the vacuum of space. So. Paul keeps walking down Vermont. Ducking through bell door ring and ordering a chicken schwarma pita.

How long does it take for frostbite to set in? At what temperature? He is sure of the frostbite. Can he even remember what fingers felt like? Shake the hands like a flapper on a wooden stage. He's been in the walk-in for hours. Grabbing at bottles of beer cola juice, fronting cartons of milk by date, sort of. Unable tell if he is holding the glass without watching the hands do it. The alcohol keeping him alive. You cant freeze whiskey and, although it sweats & scrambles to escape his body, exploding again & again inside the shattered remains of his skull, it keeps him moving.

Stepping out of the cooler, the clock on the wall showing some nonsense about only five minutes having passed. When he isn't driving he is stocking, sweeping, degreasing, moping, lubricating, carrying boxes of coffee or cream soda up tile stairs thick with beef fat, bread crust, pickle spears, dodging cooks & cleaners, the occasional falling vat of mayonnaise. He might be asked to bus tables covered in uneaten food, discarded by the rich and/or wasteful. Picky bastards who never touch half the stuff. So he'll squirrel away a pint of coleslaw, a bowl of soup, cut off the one potentially slobbery bite from a corned beef sandwich, a cold baked potato.

He gets free coffee which has its pros and cons, but besides that, the higher-ups won't let him have a toothpick. Won't even let him buy a toothpick till the end of his shift. And only then with their personal blessing for each specific item & occasion. He damn sure isn't gonna pay for meals when he works at a restaurant. So he waits for mis-orders, uneaten, or un-picked-up food, assembling the disparate parts of a meal out in the van. Perfecting methods of eating soup while driving. One handing a ruben on a sharp curve.

Some days he doesn't leave the house at all. Locking himself in the facade of a sitcom. Whole seasons pass in a day (and in the nearly singular sunny season of Los Angeles, this makes him feel productive). A bottle of rum. Sink back in the frayed edges of the easy chair, black at the elbows with slick scars of wear. The laptop screen broadcasting constant waves of escape. Innocuous opium dream, painted sentimental sweet with the soothing lacquer of spiced rum. He will watch any show or movie where people about his age seem to be moving through the world confidently or, having found their niche, moving at least without interference. Where characters have each others backs and nothing never doesn't work out in the end. After hours, mind floating wobbly, he'll remember a story, an anecdote about a friend. The glowing face, squat, starring back. But the story was about you all along, he'd laugh to the screen. Realizing his deep assimilation of episodic experience-not-his-own. The lives of its characters. His characters.

Settle back into the old easychair m'boy. Paul floating in the echo of his own voice. Rockford or Columbo, Six Pam Grier movies back to back with her fabulous tits. He'd get up to use the john. Wonder when the bed had gotten over here, he over there. Settle again in to the chair's easy embrace. On these days always settle in. The helicopters will swirl their wobbling ellipses. The ambulances bwoop & moan fading from to and from. And Paul will turn up, turn down the volume of TV music movies accordingly.

Out. The light leaves quietly through the windows.

In. Come the minstrels of night.

The screen keeps his attentions. The rum keeps him emotionally involved.

Finishing the roach he'd lit to enhance the days jerk off, re-moving his pants, laying on the bed. Slowly, deliberately, thinking only of masturbating as the act and the erotic material. Aroused by the cleansing vehicle of getting off. He may have thought about a woman here or there. Maybe even a dude, who can say in such moments? This one was just for the release. After a few minutes, eyes closed, underwear still clenching his thighs—

Buttoning his jeans in the kitchen. Turn on the coffee maker, metal plate re-heating yesterdays pot, remaining drips and drops of water in the empty reservoir hiss and pop against the metal coil as the machine vainly attempts to start its programed mechanism . Today he will kneel at the alter of the city. Let It guide him. Leaving destination up to chance with a game he plays; taking paths of least resistance. At the redline, board the first train arriving. Debark the first stop that seems appropriate (usually based on a chance to buy food or drink. gut impulse). Climb the steps of the first open bus doors you see headed N S E W. Remove into the streets at any place unfamiliar. Start walking. At intersections, always choose the crossing with no wait time (even if this causes double-backs or circles). Never stop walking 'till you do. Buy as many pints as needed to complete the journey or as cashflow & liquor store saturation dictate.

Alternate listening: albums v. the beating dry breath of the city. It's always dry here. Even in flooding deluge of raindog mon-soon, the city remains cracked and calloused. He will try to see the streets as one Fante had in the 30's, as another in the 90's. The way Chester Himes did in the 50's and Wanda Coleman in the 70's. How it's seen by others now from El Monte, Downey, Beverly Hills, Inglewood, Watts, Malibu (Lebowski), SFV, Glendale, Hollywood, Mid-City West, Down off Pico, Marina Del Ray, Pedro, Eagle Rock, Las Tunas, Hollywood Park, Santa Monica, moving through the bustle, a shirking stage hand, lost in the play. Watching our shared experience unfold in 18.679 million differently similar ways.

Brushing his teeth, plus sized silhouette of downtown loom-ing on the horizon, mounted in the window on his bathroom wall. Sunshine and smog blow in through the screen, filling the small tile room. Van Ronk's version of *Hang Me, Oh Hang Me* recycles his mind, filled with savory melancholy.

Wandering street-level, above the underground, below the stacked glass of those buildings, keeping the sun, whenever possible, at arms length. Banging from shadow to shadow to keep light and limber. Walking slowly, sips from the ass-pocket whiskey bottle between street corners, wondering what to do next. Not today- today is handled. The whiskey, the exercise, the formula. He'll stop at the Monte Cristo, the diner on 4th? 5th? Where there is always a pimp in a razorbrimmed hat, that sour skid row smell, some cat trying to light 1/2 a menthol or bum one....Not today, but tomorrow, next week, month year. What will he do then, perpetually, forever?

Crossing the street toward him- a short caballero, right foot meeting the earth, a 90° L at the ankle. Seems to put all the weight of hisself on that busted thing, hitting his stride and passing Paul at a pretty quick clip. Hardly using the cane gripped in the wrong hand, supporting the wrong leg.

Someone aught to have shown him how to use that thing, Paul thinks. But then, he would know, wouldn't he? How best for him at least. I mean, this didn't seem like a new gig for the guy. He may have even spent years toiling with that damned cane like they'd told him to. Support the bad leg with the strong auxiliary wood, smooth and defined. Until one day, beginning to step, the cane slipping on the stillwetfrompressurewashing concrete, fearing all lost, feeling the ankle bend beneath his weight and.... spring back! Propelling him forward & through his peril. Since that day he's kept handy the cane, but moves through the world with that signature shuffle and spring. This is the story Paul imagines for him. Incredible, whatever the situation, the man's ability to adapt.

Hearing a thud-hollow ring, he looks back in time to see the man bounce off a green planted mailbox, staying upright and quickly regaining top loping speed. I am surrounded by examples of perseverance. Sudden smell of menthol, head pivoting back toward his direction of travel just in time to step around a smokestack reconnoitering his bulging cart. On the other side he is greeted by glassed greasy eyes of the diner. Moving through the open face, selecting a glossy pink and white checker cracked vinyl throne, hot coffee arrives before he's even decided which section of the Times to unfurl, splayed across the counter to his right.

He likes to look at a paper in a diner. In a coffee shop, on the bus, the train, in Pershing Square, outside a theater. For the moment, printed news is no longer necessary. And because of that, and maybe since always, most of what they print is garbage. Or ads. So much fucking advertisement. But it feels connected. Vital. To read the newspaper in LA. Connected to the authors artists down but not out blue collar bums with coffee breath ink blotched nicotine stained fingers sucking on a pen, who've clicked their heels and beat the dust off every inch of concrete in this city. Warmed every park bench with their prone weariness hungry searching prayers.

Trying to watch your own eyes blink is hard. In the hat shop mirror, Paul is having no luck. A stingy maroon fedora slides down his sweaty forehead in slow cartoon trombone fashion- bbrrrrm-mmmppffff- taking it off and leaning forward to the fan, the loud wind's motor sucking electric current, holding the sweat beads to their cooling intentions.

By 4o'clock he's drunk. Has finished a pint and wandered into a few saloons, ordering a double at each, draining the amber hot calamity before it hit the bar. Wandering back out. He likes the way this makes bartenders look at him. A legend in his own mind. Here is a man who knows what he wants, wants it straight, drinks quick, leaves a tip, and moves back out into the aimless queue of people choking the streets.

Stay away from crowded bars. Where he is always overlooked, or ignored. Never able to figure out which or why. Don't these people know he is a serious man, with serious need for a drink? Don't they know he can get a bottle anywhere? (Maybe they do, and that is the problem) But he'll stand there, raising a hand— probably really a finger, to look cooler, not some over eager 5th grader who wants some milk— every time the bartender makes a move. Hoping to catch their attention. These bartenders, men & women, seem capable of doing their jobs without a glance in whatever direction Paul chose to stand. Move to the area where their attention seems directed? They move to where he'd just been. Leaving him to watch his reflection dissolve ad infinitum.

Just when he's decided to leave, they ask- what'll it be? Impatient, as if they are doing him a favor. So he'll order his drink, pound it & leave a good tip. Having really shown them. He is Paul Trune, serious drinker. A man of the world. A man who works for a living. A blue collar roustabout raconteur, not one of these two faced dreamers with exaggerated screen credits and a headshot in every pocket. So they take his money like they don't give a shit who he is and wander off to shake the hands and slap the backs of all the cool kids.

Standing in a strip of shade smoking after draining a beer at Grand Central Market, thinking about the better luck he has with some bartenders. Black, female barkeeps, seem to be the most supportive of his indulgences. White men the worst. He loves strong women. And broken ones. All of the kinds. With two scoop bodies of ice cream licked smooth, bulging in all the right places.

In the midst of this reverie his phone rings. Where are you? He can barely hear the voice over rushing cars. Downtown. Whats up? He is shouting. You were s'pposed to be here an hour ago. His mind wandering in a thousand directions. Shit. What day is it? Am I on the schedule? The voice telling him about covering a shift. I forgot that was this week. I'll see you in an hour.

It will take at least an hour to get to the deli in Hollywood. He'll have to stop in K-Town to get his work gear; a button down shirt and a couple'a airplane bottles to keep the hangover from kicking in till after midnight. Heading across the street to the redline station below Angels Flight. Passing the steep staircase to Bunker Hill, wondering how many times Richard Valenzuela or Chico Hamilton or some ginned up pinstriped zoot had traversed this path. He's late for work and feels bad about it. Lately, the drink, well, it feels like he's been gotten hold of. It hadn't always been like this. For fifteen years he'd never taken a drink before work. Well, a few times. But on those rare occasions he'd still been on time and able to function.

But fifteen years is a long time. A lifetime of worrying about job security. Even when there was security, worrying about whether there'd be enough money. And what about savings? Who are these people who can afford to save? Paul is a white man in a white man's world and is barely treading water. He can't even imagine life without a cock, or skin a darker shade. Besides the drinks, which can add up, but are mostly cheap when he stays out of bars, he has no real expenditures. Outside of rent and utilities, food, the occasional book or magazine, he rarely buys anything. Bus fare. No new clothes or shoes, no fancy dinners or vacations. Maybe this is his own damned fault. For never applying himself, never wanting for much. Now working class poverty, living paycheck to paycheck, is second nature. Always afraid everything is falling apart.

Even if it does, he can always move back with his folks. Back to the whitewashed suburbs. He can ask them for money. Has in the past. Not that they have much. But they've always been supportive. Always forgiving. He keeps giving them the pain they seem to need. Maybe he hates them for that. For always being there. Him never having to fight too hard. He thinks he's grateful. But who knows.

There's nothing really wrong in his world. So what is the constant gnawing? Is his every god dammed action self sabotaging? Drunk or sober he can't get it right. His parents will die. Then what? Will he be forever at the mercy of the kindness of strangers. After his friends have all deserted him, or he them (a path he's a ways into already), will he be a drunk munching a discarded peach, reclaimed from a bus stop trash can?

Under the humid lights of the train, feeling in every pore a coward. Life in this way seems unsustainable. But he's grown so accustomed to it. Any other method feels like watching someone else's dream. Always trying to take the path of least resistance seems to have gone sideways on him. Like turning off the light without getting out of bed. Using more energy once, having realized the switch is out of reach, you determine to succeed based on principal.

He is so full of hatreds he can no longer differentiate. After years of careful study he is brimming with them. So much that if the little cells bobbing and dying in the booze saw something besides hate they would fail to recognize it. Self hate, world hate, hating drink, hating dry. Anger, frustration, loathing. He has combed his world, curating the finest and most complete collection of negative adjectives, clinging tightly and defining himself through them. So precisely tuned to helpless, hopeless, and never knowing it. Really believing that he is a lover of life, frantically thinking, if only more people were like him. He drinks himself to a state of nothingness. Down to the bottom of an endless pit where everything ceases. And when the hate is gone, when everything is gone to nothing, when the poison has finally silenced the beast, he passes out. Not from the liquor, but from the body forgetting its function in the absence of all that familiar rage.

Hating this job, the manager, most of the employees and customers. Hates the Dicksboro, his neighbors, the bums with their constant need. He hates everyone and everything and holds his nose up high in disapproval and superiority. He is lost and broken. He knows this in most moments and so feels powerless. If he is to accept this as truth, which pains him, then he must face the pain. And the fear. If he allows himself to believe in something different, then things might change. What if they don't change into what he dreams? What if they do? What if he is forever lost?

That time I got the pictures. The 3rd time. Out on the beach in St. Petersburg Florda, Sal continues, dragging a cigarette, ashing. Talking about encounters. The like-always conspiracies and strange goings on that weave their constant thread through all his conversations. The camera broke on me. But I got the film developed and there she was, big as life. I was coming down from some heavy acid but no, for real, a triangular ship with blue lights. Like headlights. You know what I mean? And five F-18's flankin' her. Pictures in a box somewhere. At my old man's house I think.

For the last ten minutes Sal's been really pushin' the idea that he has definitive proof of extra terrestrial, uber advanced technologically superior space ship flyin' mother fuckin' aliens, that he is keeping in a box somewhere. Paul can listen, or at least half listen, for hours. Never ceasing to be amazed by the elaborately concocted, convoluted streams of analysis.

I mean, the CIA's been able to bend time since the sixties. Just check online. It's well documented. One of the first technologies they gave us when they showed up in recent years. Of course, they were here before. The pyramids, which there are more of than we know, Atlantis, Stonehenge. Sister cities with unaccountably similar deities and rituals. I've got a book you can borrow. The nature of god in the Egyptian language. Exploring the definitive narratives in ancient text proving the existence of visitors.

Killing the last cold slug of coffee, Paul drops his cigarette in the ashtray. My attorney… Sal had switched subjects at some point. Seamlessly swimming along the periphery of Paul's consciousness. Well I got this guy… he tells me we've got a good case. Tells me I said and did all the right things. I made it seem like he'd come on to me, my boss. I mean he kinda did. He's a prick anyways. Me and this other dude he called a nigger. This lawyer guy says we can take him in court. Maybe 30 grand each. Pro'lly less but not by much. 20 minimum. Till then, I'll just play it fast and loose, with the other stuff I got goin'…. I'm meeting with that producer this week. That friend, he's like a mentor really, took me under his wing when I first got out here, produced records for Hendrix and Cream and shit, he's a fuckin wizard man on the board, been clean now 30 days, he's gonna get me in the studio on tape, still friends with Mitch, Mitch Mitchell man, they lived in a crack house together, he's gonna get us on tape, and there're some gigs here and there, people, most people just aren't ready for the truth though, watching that t.v.- herd advertising subliminal agenda pepsi cola bullshit- like Atlantis, how they found it off the coast of Spain and nobody even gives a shit. They just wanna dream their preprogrammed dreams beamed down on microwaves, downloaded from space, chemtrails, saw some the other night, Wednesday, above the church at Fountain and Fairfax, the cloud man, put your life in the cloud, eye in the sky, upload your content... Can I borrow your phone?"

Sal walks outside with the phone, leaving Paul on the broken down couch, a VHS tape of Jaco Pastorius buzzing its grainy frames of pastel 80's hue on the old 13" Panasonic Tape Combo. Reach for the compact metal pipe on the table to take a whistling slow resin hit, leftover ash glowing its last as fading embers cling to metal screen and the flame hot air mixed smoke dips down his throat. He admires Sal in a way, is frightened of him. Of becoming him. His single mindedness without a glimmer of hope. Mid-thirties, divorced (Paul can tell he loves his kids, they mean the world, and all the other inhabited planets, to him. But Sal is no father and Paul suspects they both know that), unhealthy on again off again relationship with a drunk chick who plays a cartoon character on the Blvd and pays all the bills, looking for the next opportunity/scam/deal/big thing, working hard in all the wrong ways, networking with deadbeats and frauds, gift of gab, a talking head.

He'd once actually told Paul that this is his last chance. If I don't make it now its over, any kinda fame would do, once you're a name you're a name for life. There's always a spot on the marquee for a name. You could see the conviction in his eyes, the way his whole body seemed clenched at the prospect. It seems to Paul that he's already another casualty. Sal loves the music, but has fallen prey to all the cliched hype. Caught in the web he condemns, he can only blame outside forces for his failure. Punks, mods, hippies, hipsters, beats, bebopers, doo wopers, chicanos, panthers, each new cultural launch followed by an explosion, a proliferation, exploitation, then ashes. In his dash to escape a societal cage, Sal wound up in some different corporate/media mass produced uniform, passing out new propaganda and marching orders. Blind to a new prison with limits of its own.

Not that Paul is any different or better. Not like he isn't on his own trip, slogging back and forth, to and from work, drinking too much free coffee, too much cheap and over priced booze. Trying to be someone he isn't sure how to be. He's here, in the same place as Sal, doing the same things as him. Under the circumstances, in these moments, they are the same. He stands, an urge to run. Sits again. Realizing he's high, ripped back to the dusty thin upholstery of the couch, semi-dark, thick/warm smell of the little living room with the stripper pole near the stereo.

Every now and then there's a party and some of the girls from the Seventh Veil- across the street its neon constellations and flash wink starlight beckoning a certaintypeoftheatercrowd- will come over and do blow. Usually reaching some unsustainable crescendo before things subside with a gong-like fade or shatter into a temporary chaos that will be retold with ever more reminiscence as the years pass, the girls changing occasionally, their pinprick pupils remaining the same.

Sal loves to be in the mix. Paul watching him surge around the room, conversations with revolving faces, a kind of Truman Show-esque display that thinks the world is watching. But he is not some pompous character of elitism who holds court as a parrot, regurgitating half-baked NPR Art 101. He is a student of his own patchwork lesson plan, a conspiracy theorist, a father, a musician, a doper, a million second string characters with a heart, however muddied or misplaced. He seems to be near the truth, his own truth at least, but there is something, maybe too many drugs, too many times he felt poised to strike gold only to come up with painted turds, some misguided course constantly skirting the edge of destination. A legend in his own mind, like Paul, primed to loom in the minds of others. If he could just get a shot. Sal re-enters the apartment, ejecting the tape, since faded to black then white snow at some point.

Folding a paper towel for a filter, pouring clumps of powdery grounds into the small Black & Decker coffee maker, scent of sweet acid earth clings to Paul's mustache. Sal packs and hits the metal pipe, motioning Paul to his turn, smoke punched deep in his lungs, holding his breath as he flips through records, stopping to fill the room with cough dancing clouds that seek out rays of light penetrating the shuttered windows, mingling deep into the corners with the smell of coffee now percolating.

How do I get here here? Paul thinks at least once each time they hang. What are we doing? he asks, expecting no reply. There is plenty of good music, Sal is generous with his weed and coffee, sometimes too much drama, always late, usually interesting, sometimes bitchy, never easy to get in touch or along with (which is why he only hangs out when Sal initiates, usually meaning that he needs something). Basically, as good a friend as you can expect. But their whole philosophies seem in opposition.

Even the way they like the same music is different. It seems that Sal filters everything through anger, punch-drunk and swinging, throwing rage and self pity and fear at the whole kit and caboodle. He can see it in Sal easier than in himself, but with himself, he thinks at least that he is looking for a way out. Has to find a way out, a way off this savage island of his own making, self fulfilling prophesies with tragic rambling endings. Years spent in search of greater pain. Pain to treat pain to treat pain. Where was the spring for this well of torment? Maybe a more impoverished upbringing would have spurred him toward greater success. Though he suspects not. More discipline then, for too long he's gotten off relatively scot-free. But looking back, no. He just redesigns the plays, accounting for interference.

You need a chick, Sal would say. Someone not too steady but stable. Someone long term he can kick the tires on. But he knows he can't put his shit on someone else. Knows he'll have to reckon with those devils in himself first. But how? Without becoming some preachy smiling Tony Robbins type fucker. He doesn't want that never ending wellspring of bumpersticker mantras. Maybe he does need a chick . One from a Lou Reed tune. Some defined female presence that's all hips lips tits hair and sex, a head full of strong feminist opinions, a bad bitch, a tortured soul, breath like wine, who late night diner drinking black coffee reads quiet from a small red notebook matching lips her treatise on life. A Lydia Davis, Ida Lupino, Kathleen Hanna, fucks where and when she wants to type.

Over the phone there'd been good conversation. Common ground. Standing in front of some jive-swank bar on Sunset pondering into a cigarette when she walked up. More full figured than her profile pictures let on. Same old story. He wonders if he would have gotten this far if the image had been more accurate. Less of a bow to the sexploitation of women in pop culture. He likes curvy women, so it isn't much of an issue, but it bothers him that he was disappointed with his initial impression. Bothers him that she felt the need to present herself in a different light. Bothers him that he is thinking any of this as she withdraws her kiss, allowing him to exhale the last drag of his cigarette.

She's 27. Korean born in Hawaii. Her heart shaped face daubed and etched with a little too much dark makeup. A punk rock chick in fishnets. She calls herself Ruby Supreme after the character in the Blondie tune.

20 min in, things are going well. No shortage of conversation. They agree the joint is subpar. She tells Paul about her father. About going back to school, about her job as a nanny to a good rich family and their good rich kids. Tells him about living in Long Beach and commuting to Hollywood. Then she tells him about living with cancer. About tumors & cysts & polyps lining the walls of her uterus. About surgeries. About being diagnosed at 15. The full time job of it. The physical and emotional drain. Living with death insider her (as we all are, he tries to forget). Remission. Explosion of cannibalistic cells. Fitting in doctors visits between school and working two jobs. Or really, fitting life between doctor visits.

He tries hard to sip his drink slowly. Not to be indelicate. Tries to talk. Use the right words. To say the least surreal things under very surreal conditions. Trying to stay open minded, but, is this a whole scenario he wants to invite into his life? He can hardly support himself emotionally, let alone this woman with another world of worries. But is that how he wants to be? To run from what seems like a real connection? Or the closest thing he's felt to something like one in a while?

Maybe it's out of narcissism that he decides to give it a go. Maybe it's Ruby's attitude. So well adjusted. So accepting of the reality, unwilling to accept some inevitability. Maybe he thinks he needs an example of that in his life. Maybe it's just that they're drunk. That he's spent over a hundred bucks on drinks and hopes he can get a screw out of it. Or that she put on a dress & makeup and came out to drink and smoke cigarettes with him, after leaving the doctors that afternoon. Not content to cling to life, or let death slowly steal. She is raw. Unapologetic. Vibrating.

On the way to his house they make it to a liquor store just in time for last call. Trying his best to give'r directions before they miss the turns. Wondering if she's as drunk. Trying to get the keys in the door to his building. Trying to get the keys into the door to his apartment. Trying to get to a light switch. Her laughing and bumping the walls behind him.

Long Beach. In a bed dripping piles of blankets, comforters, pillows, sleep. Sticky morning body hungover. Paul had taken the blue line out the night before. Getting off somewhere to board a bus, confused streets milling with people. Tank top wearers, flip flop slappers, out in force to enjoy the Long Beach Grand Prix. The bus stopping every minute. Doors opening to a flood of directional inquiries.

When he got to Ruby's building and found the apartment, she met him with wet hands and the smell of hot food wandering over the threshold. The fried sweet stench of marinated meat. Runt black cat dragging along the baseboards.

They ate Korean BBQ. White sticky rice & meat, rolled in leaves of red lettuce, dunked in some style of kimchee-ish sauce. Sitting on the floor, at the foot of her bed, a short black table, legs underneath. Drinking whiskey, Paul looking around at the walls & bookcases. Talking. The phone rings. Yes. Yes. Shut up. Yes, I do. A guy I know. No. You cant. His name is Paul. I'll talk to you tomorrow. Yes I know. You saw through the kitchen window. I did tell him.

That was my friend Shawna, she reported. She saw you through the kitchen window because she lives over there and she's nosey. Pointing at a glowing orange square across the courtyard, the blinds wide. She does hair at a salon in Beverly Hills, but she used to work at a different salon that was owned by my boss now, that I used to work for in Culver City. She moved in here about three years ago and she wants me to tell her all about you. And she wanted to come over right now but I told her I'd talk to her tomorrow. But she's really nice. I think you'd like her.

They watched 'Crumb' in bed. They fucked on the floor, for one reason or another, to Johnny Shines banging out his notes in call or response. Music for things that go bump in the night. Then Paul sat on the carpet facing the wall. In the room with the music carpet cat lingering smell of sugary meat woman music stale air plastic cup full o' butts dirty dishes torsos feet limbs. By the beach, sort of. Everything seemed OK. Indoors. Satiated by food, sex, the tight squish of a big bed. Near sunrise the day seemed far away. So many moments. He drank some whiskey. Running a tongue over teeth like seashells plump & wet, adding a cigarette to a butt cup, he sank into bed.

Untangling from the mass of sheets, goodbye, moving out

the door, stepping along morning sidewalk Long Beach, 6:30am. Walking the reverse route of last night. The morning still and grey, violently throbbing through his body. Walking starting to loosen him up. With brain pounding he stops to get the biggest bottle of water available. Plenty of time before work, his clean uniform clothes & deodorant bundled in the backpack. Hydrate and relax. Read on the train. Relax. Enjoy the calming fruits of a night well spent in the world. Wine women song. The hangover grind of a conquering hero. An artist who refuses to live by the rising & setting of the sun. A man fully immersed in the human experience, wringing the pain & joy from toil & beauty & madness. He's a long way from those aimless teenage days of suburb parking lot skateboards. But is he?

Christ, a few hours sleep would be nice. Some coffee & Advil at the deli. Maybe he'll make good tips. Hoping there won't be any large deliveries, but all far away. With big tips. So he's out all day, driving, not standing around on the uneven tiles, stocking, carrying shit, trying to look busy. Some of these long distance jobs could net $25/30 tip each. Couple'a those....

Push through the heavy wood door- 30 min early. Pour a coffee & look in vain for an under-the-counter aspirin. Exit out back to sit on one of the bowed milk crates hedging a corner of the parking lot. Smoking, listening to Sunset Blvd. Heaving with something like life.

In this age of text and email and endless connectivity we all have to think about what someone will answer, before we even formulate the question/statement, including that potential answer and any others into our original equation and….. No. Never mind. At first, Paul thought he'd hit on some new psychological social malady. Something to make him understand why the world & everyone in it seems so crazy. But the problems of the first world are not new problems. They are exponentially evolving, based on the technology of the times. We've been dealing with these things since the dawn of human interaction.

Still, maybe some temperance or all out revolt against these tendencies of analysis could be beneficial? Maybe. Or maybe that is lunatic behavior. Living with no filter. That's what his drinking is. Maybe. Some green light & gas pedal strapped to the feet of an emotional cripple. Is he so thoroughly entrenched in identifying as a bohemian, a drunk hardboiled wrecking ball of a man? Can he even call himself a man? Never mind the image presented. He still sees himself as a child. At most a teen. Sees other people see him as such. Paul has built himself into a corner. Into this caricature, fulfilling all the promises, pictures, interviews, of the people he's spent a lifetime emulating. Wanting so badly to be like. Without noticing, he has become his imitations. But what to do when you get here and realize how unhappy all those bastards were? How many died before they got one breath of clean air?

Again catching his attention, watching through the window of the Dicksboro lobby, the man on the phone who'd sparked his earlier contemplations. Man holding a personalized world in the palm of his hand. Pictures, thoughts, phone numbers, secret alternate online realities, bank accounts, pictures of his cock, of women or men with his cock. A specific & safe escape. Like Paul's apartment. With its pictures & music & daydreams & nudity. Anonymity.

Only one generation has really experienced the crossover into the galaxy of the cell phone. Maybe 2. The mobile phone, and it's further iterations, has done more for lonely people than anything in history. It may also have created more lonely people than ever before. People who didn't know they were lonely until given the opportunity of constant, minute by minute update on how un-alone everyone else is. Although mostly this is a scam, an aggrandizement perpetrated by everyone, all of us lonely, wondering about our purpose, to produce the facade of a busy, adventurous life, full of death defying feats, beautiful people, events, misquotes of philosophical principals from books never read, etc.

Busy people, rich people, those with places to do and people to be, don't need cell phones. It's a person outside 7-Eleven; smoking in a car with the windows down, longing for a comrade, for an ass in the passenger seat, with no destination, moving from parking lot to parking lot, bar to bar to diner, needing someone to voice doubts to, or jokes, a companion with whom to share observational humor, a sounding board, who needs the ability to make contact.

Now they've pulled out all the dirty phone booths, or at least ripped out the receivers, sickly wires dripping. Leaving patchwork skeletons of graffiti & stickers with trash jammed and stacked on or in every orifice. Recently he'd seen a photo book called *Every Payphone on Sunset Boulevard* and found himself thinking of all the not too far off days of feeding quarters (maybe even dimes as a kid, he couldn't quite recall) into those greasy PacBell boxes. In his youth, dialing 1-800-WET-TITS outside the drugstore, listening to the prerecorded lusty throbbing voice of a probably 50 year old smoker with sagging juggs, and feeling a tingle & a sense of shame somewhere. Do kids still find porn & jackoff in the woods. It feels like there was a lot more semi-public sexual discovery when he was growing up. Maybe he was just a fucking pervert, and maybe it's better that kids aren't finding used porn in gutters & trashcans or learning how to fuck from the lavender/green stuttering feed of channel 99 late night softcore.

He doesn't want to come across as some vintage nostalgia, what's the internet, I only listen to vinyl blowhard, but it seems like there was some greater sense of wonder, some dirty raw connection between people back then. A lively electric current that could be tapped unintentionally, when you least expected connectivity, resulting in an unplanned, unrepeatable experience. A less diluted reality. Or maybe not diluted, but less tailor made.

Maybe this guy is texting his kid on a different coast, or his mother, next to his fathers hospital bed. It isn't all worthless. He could be emailing vocal tracks to a musical collaborator in Africa, or learning about local government and police corruption. He could be doing anything really. Looking at a video of a monkey riding a dog or a person being fucked by a horse. There are a lot of animals on the internet.

You can eat eggs 2 days past the date on the carton. Right? He makes sure it's sell by: not use by: and cracks them into the smoking oil. Fries the tortillas in the remnants, and smashes some room temp refried beans on the plate. He likes the cool beans against the hot running eggs and tortillas. Handful of black olives on the side. Hot coffee & a cold jug of water.

No one ever talks about the drinking of water that goes along with the constant consumption of alcohol. Or the fact that some days you cant drink. Days when you can't get any. When you're alone and it's too much to stand. So you clutch at the bed in the most fetal of positions, wishing you could sink inside some soft comfort where the pins & needles stop their constant prodding. Some old embryonic stage before all the trouble & decision making. All the dealing with things. And the water. Maybe he's alone in this, but there's never enough water in the world to make it right. Each piss looking less like whiskey getting him that much farther from the edge of death.

Today is not one of those days. He tries to remember this feeling. Its OK-ness. Will try to remember to remember it. Sitting at the wood table. Mopping up eggs and beans in the window.

Everyone is depraved/deranged in a way that is specific to themselves. What we fantasize about is our depravity. Something we are not doing now, or not doing enough, or knowing that we shouldn't do. What a churchgoer and a pornstar think is depraved will be different. Each even existing only as a rebellion against the other. Neither right or wrong. Even the extremists are right. If everything can exist, eventually it must. The internet is proof enough of that. But if we each have that which we consider depraved, the thing that rubs against the moral fibre of our being, then we also have the polar opposite of that. The thing we know is higher than us. The greater.

Scrubbing himself with the luffa. Practically skinning himself. Feeling great, engulfed in steam. He thinks people think luffas are for women and gay men. Women and gay men have great ideas about hygiene he thinks. Wouldn't mind doing some of those bath bomb relaxer things sometime.

Not that the depraved is necessarily wrong, it certainly appeals to our more animal side and there is something to be argued in listening to some of our more basic impulses, but maybe there is more to be gained by increasing the frequency of reaching toward those higher gains. The inclusive. When someone is calm, pleasant, well mannered, well spoken, offering assistance, what do we think if not worldly, well traveled, open, accepting, diverse.

Maybe instead of constantly falling prey to his baser instincts, his personal needs, he can focus on the needs of others, or on acting the way he thinks people should act in the world. Looking beyond himself, because nothing affects him really. There are two states: 1. Living 2. Dead, so nothing affects him when he is living, 'cause he's still just living, and nothing affects him when he's dead, 'cause he's still just dead.

What do I need to build a couch? Some sweet opium den type job. Think I can do it. Some wood, cushion, fabric, a youtube video. If I do a good job, replace the cover and cushions every 10/15 years, it could last a lifetime. Like grandma did. She didn't build the stuff, but replaced the innards and outerds, depression era upbringing. There are at least ten different ways to do it. Designs. Practical application and process. How to upholster, 3" cushion foam, unobtrusive seams, wooden legs? Height? There is no need for a new couch. And if I want one there are plenty of thrift store/curbside deals that cost less in materials & man power. None of my tools are easily accessible, and other than my parents house, I have no real place to do the labor. Then my dad will want to help. What's so wrong with that? He's a good carpenter. Much better than me. He won't be around forever. Once he's gone, dead, candles out, I'll wish we had more time together. The same way he felt when his father died. Years of should have's. I never can guess how I'll react to my parents deaths. Thinking I love them, but never sure what that means. Not a thing you can be sure about, until they disappear maybe. They have been constant. The oldest feelings I have, bad or good. They've shaped me in ways I'll never know. The same way I'll never really know who they were as people, outside and beyond me. The years they spent being these people I can't see them as. Having only recently realized that my parents really have lived lives, I feel like an idiot for all the doubt I've had toward their advice over time. Realizing after years of hearing it, that they wrestled with the same demons and more, that I have. Houses and mortgages, loss & gain, an alchy son bidding his time, making trouble. Everything growing & crumbling and replacing, shouting a countdown louder through the years.

When it went 5-3 after they scored, i'm so happy bro, i mean it's going so good, when they went 5-3 i cried, i cried bro, you know what i mean?

This conversation cycles in from somewhere, causing his eyes to open, erasing the dream. Paul doesn't know what these words mean and doesn't care. Has forgotten where he is. Thinking the man must be talking about sports but... The voice is coming from the corridor. This is his room. That is the world. He is awake, in the world, happy to be part of it, happier that he is currently locked away against it. Here in his space, his rules, his things.

Waking up next to Shanne for the second time in as many months. Take a pull off the bottle of peppermint Schnapps that lays between them, immediately regretting it. Memories of last night already beginning to piece themselves together. The painful, ego-crushing part when he'd tried to fuck her. Did fuck her for a bit. Working away at it till she'd voiced concerns about this affecting their work relationship, or maybe she was embarrassed, maybe turned off, maybe never turned on. Found him disgusting. She hadn't been screaming, there was no hitting, nothing of a forced nature he could remember. Nothing forced, besides his need to fuck, his need to force himself into the preprogramed mold of man as sexual conquistador, forced by his perceptions and the rhetoric of societal norms.

A fleeting sense of calm, unable to remember being rapey. Doesn't think he'd raped her. The fact that he is grappling with this distinction however, seems an immediate cause for alarm. He can only assume the worst from blackouts. Even if there is no evidence, no precedent for his worries. All this running through his head, her body half under, half hanging naked from beneath the sheets. All this running through his head last night, pulling himself in & out of her, as hard as he could get after all the booze, her face calm during penetration as she gave support to her hypothesis that they shouldn't be fucking. So he'd rolled off, panting, and now they're here.

She wakes slowly, stretching, asking for a swig off the Schnapps. He offers a cigarette which she declines, then takes from his lip, her face pickled, throat wheezy gasp from the peppermint poison. Should he apologize? Always afraid of being an asshole, seeming always to be one regardless. She hadn't run off, or cursed him, or cut his dick off while he slept. That's a good sign. Take a drag from the schnapps, almost vomiting. Why does she drink this shit?

Shanne tells him not to worry. They're friends, adults, drunk, these things happen. He asks for a kiss. Can they try again then? No. She laughs, taking the bottle with her to the shower. Paul sitting, smoking, head turned to the window, ashing in an empty coke bottle near the bed, starring out the portholes of his fortification. Trying to smell the sex, if any lingers in the room.

They cross Berendo to Saver Liquor for a pint of breakfast whiskey. She'd finished the Schnapps in the shower, and suggested that they spend the day together, platonically. Paul is grateful. For her company, her strength. She is understanding, Shanne. Empathic. Or maybe fucked in the head for putting up with him. He isn't sure he even wanted to fuck her. He probably did, but mostly booze has always been enough. Sure he's been with a few women, but it's mostly something to chase after like everything else. People always wanting to know, are you getting some? When was the last time? TV ads, movies, books, art, everything tits and ass, chiseled abs and jaw lines, eat this drink this buy this GET FUCKED! There must be something to it, else why would it be so prevalent in conversation, marketing, history? All the greats had had hordes of women/men. Even his parents wanted to know, family members, Are you seeing anyone? People over the years had thought him gay. Fine. He can't see what business it is of theirs. Then they wonder, Where are the men in his life?

But it's tough. Out there. In the world. Meeting people. Women. Trying to keep upright. Like everything else you have to put in some effort. Put up some kind of front. He imagines, even with groupies, you have to live up to some image/persona of the false idol they've been mentally constructing. It's all so much work. The theatrics. A bottle requires nothing, offering itself up for any occasion. You don't even need money really. But it seems easier for Paul to work a bit & have a few comforts, than to duke it out in the gristle of the streets.

Night. He can't remember how he'd spent the day with Shanne. When she'd left or what they'd done. When did they get back to the apartment? Remember walking. Remember the sun. Remember the blackness and swim in the empty space of it. Directionless. Feel heavy muscles motionless, breathless on the bed, starring through the ceiling. Still. Not to disturb the resting calm of the box of objects around him. Focus on the vibration of the room.

There is a bottle on the floor. Well, there are a few, but only one worth attending to. He'll pound at it like he had Shanne the night before; half heartedly till he passes out. Waking through the night to quench his thirst and quiet his dreams.

Running a block. Walking. Quickly. Run. Walk. Feeling burning, exploding, collapsing. Walk. Run. It's 30 minutes past when he would have been late, and after the recent suspicions about his on the job sobriety he can't allow himself to keep slipping, for them to see him slipping. Can't let them see the hangover that's really just a waning drunk. Can't let himself be seen.

The building enters view near the top of the last hill and he can feel his pace slow dramatically. Trying to organize, compose, arrange. Doubled over now, body taking control, mind oblivious, retching. Compose. Passing on the far side of the street and crossing, stopping to buy a Gatorade, a V8 and a pack of camels, taking a piss, washing his face, dragging room temp water through perspiring hair. Looking through the mirror.

Down the liquids and smoke half a square crossing the parking lot. He is in it. Spiraling down to that familiar ecosystem, the swelling sound meeting his descent. He is face to face with it. And everything is looping along as it always does, the things going wrong the way the always do, and someone plucking him up and setting him to a task with a perfunctory comment on his tardiness before, finally seeing him, asking, why are you so wet?

There are 27 surveillance cameras in and around this building, today he will spend his time avoiding all of them. And yet, it will feel like they have never taken their steady eyes off him. He knows the way these days go, has developed something akin to a trick knee that can tell the weather, over the years, through the jobs. Then he's hit with the good news. The gospel according to Saint Joseph. Has to ask for verification. Relief. The boss is out of the office for the rest of the day. Feel himself go calm. The authoritative figure who's presence so deeply troubles him, has granted a shift of reprieve. Things will remain chaotic, there will still be work, but a paralyzing tenseness he had not even noticed, has been removed.

Somewhere off Rossmore all is lost. I have been driving aimlessly for two hours. The map, stare at it, change the angle, none of it makes sense anymore. Lost track of how much whiskey I've had. Driving around with one eye closed to force out the double vision. Glad to be in a clearly marked delivery vehicle. As long as I can keep it together the cops won't hassle me. But I'll have to give up soon. Have to head back. Can't find the place. So many missed calls from work as I hold the phone, unable to answer, unable to formulate thought. Resignedly unwrapping a sandwich, stomach clenches and I throw it back in the bag. Instinctually trying to clear the empty bottles from the car, gearing up for the drive back to work, tired and confused. Run my hands slowly through sticky hair, pulling them down my greasy face, bracing. Dumb luck, eyes focusing at the right moment and I see it. The address hidden behind an overgrown bougainvillea clinging to the building. Pulling myself together. Buzzed in dramatically. Enter the foyer. The elevator stuck. Between the 12 & 14 floors. 2 gallons of chicken matzo ball soup cooling. Blackness. Glowing numbered orbs float, placing themselves in perfectly symmetrical rows, forming an illustrated box around me. Burning shadows crawl back into themselves. A light, first I hear the buzzing current, a bulb glows illuminating, placing me in the middle of an elevator. Suddenly a heave up, a jolt down. I drop the food. This continues. Up down. I am change in a tin can. Down up. There is a mechanism malfunctioning, I look to the ceiling expecting to see an air vent, little pieces of plastic tinsel or string billowing there. There is only ceiling. I am worried I will faint. I am trapped. The elevator is trapped. We are caught in one of several esophageal tracts of the building. I am pressing all the buttons and each one disappears after a ding that takes us nowhere. I am smoking now. Thick choking smoke and I am unfazed. There is a crack and I wait to fall. I am eating hot soup. The cigarette is out but the steam from the plastic container, the steam pours past my lips as I take down one matzo ball after the other. The steam and the smoke, "we will burn ourselves out!" I shout to no one. We will die in here. Trapped. For no goddamn reason. We shouldn't even be here. The elevator car continues to jolt-lurch-creep between the two floors.

Cold air whips the inside of the van, slowly called back from a dream by the ringing phone. Turn off the A/C, upright the seat. The phone rumbles in the plastic cup holder, answer, an indistinguishable voice on the other end, the short jagged questions are a deep throbbing pain, pulse quick beating the pattern of his vision. They are summoning, he is being summoned. Called back to the old building, the framework that threatens, though he gets the impression that not for much longer, to trap him, to dissect him, turning him into a thing for them to use. A thing to be used. Swimming in sweat, checking the road and funneling shakily into the flow of traffic trying to get his bearings, to keep from popping.

Back at the deli, soup down the front of his shirt, Paul hands over the keys to the van without a word. They tell him he's done. Unemployed. Ask him what he was doing, what is he on? Tell him how lucky that they hadn't called the cops, reported him. Say nothing. Nothing to say. Can't explain how he doesn't understand it himself. Hang the apron, say nothing to no one. Step slowly, don't give yourself away, the only thought he has. His mantra. Repeat. Walking Sunset with the little glass bottles, empty twinkling in his pocket. Into the Liquor Locker. Buy a pint of vodka to sit on the bus bench and pull. Waiting for the 218 down Crescent Heights, a farewell ride.

He's gotten himself to a state of constantly redistributed fear. Each month week day hour, from second to second, talking himself down from one ledge only to find himself clinging to another of equal or greater terror. Convinced for no reason he has AIDS, running the statistics from the internet, now sure that he has some type of std. Because if he doesn't have one, it'll be diabetes from all the drinking. Or cancer, or the spiders that have surely laid eggs inside his body as he sleeps. Or the constant threat of homelessness.

He's read so many of the books about coming to terms with the human condition. Tried meditation, prayer, Buddhism, Hinduism, all the novels about suffering, all the music. Is it just plain guilt about being alive? Fear of the known and unknown equally? Is he poisoning himself with theoretical material along with the physical poisons of his day to day? Or is it that he abandons all these changes before they can take hold? Alighting to another at the slightest wafting breeze of oncoming discomfort. When had the self assured boy turned into this sniveling coward of a man? He cannot rectify the way he sees himself with the cool cucumber front he peddles to the rest of the world.

Try using some of the tactics he's aware of to convince himself of his own validity, but to seemingly no avail. He is lost and helpless in this cycle. His emotional stability, or lack there of, becoming ever more fragile. A constant cluster of nerves on the verge of tears or laughter, usually in opposition to the correct reaction. Listening to lonely sorrowful songs. Watching bleak desolate movies. Alone with his thoughts as he's always been. Thoughts that come across as a calamity to most. And the ones he shares are usually his most positive or benign. The things that make him yearn and strive, his reasons for living.

So he has only himself. But that is how it's always been. An only child. Whose parents, however much they tried, had never understood. Those early childhood friends, long gone on different paths. Sometimes he sat in silence, trying to clear his mind, to remember those names and faces from the past. Nothing. What had they ever had in common? And if there were shared truths, how could they have ended up so differently? Not that he knew if any of these people were better off, he was beginning to think no one was better off than anyone else. Our lives are, however they are. Our personally perceived struggles the same.

He must make choices. Positive choices. To hustle for something. To hustle double time, to make up for all these years of anti-hustle. In younger days, sure he was destined for greatness. Not a doubt nor plan. But what to be great at? And so doubt had crept in, a roach through the torn screen. It lay in bed spoon feeding gloppy sweet opium to his motivation. Just a little at first to calm the fear. And slowly the habit grew. Quietly weaving a cocoon of isolation and anger and self hate. Even in moments of clarity, waking and finding himself mid encasement, laying quietly, offering himself up, before going back to sleep.

So he spent his hours and days and years. Emerging now, an underdeveloped creature of no worth. But, he can almost believe it's not to late. He can do something. Maybe the the secret is in the daily striving. The struggle of how to be, equal to the struggle of how not to be. The struggle against sweet opium leaking her way back in. Those calm dreams of complacency wheedling away the drive, the ambition. Or is the answer a balance between collective anonymity, and growth/evolution for the benefit of the collective whole.

Turning off the shower, running hands over hair, ringing out the water, knowing that it's probably good he's not yet achieved any degree of wealth or notoriety. Those things would have killed him a couple'a times over. He is a crooked cigarette. Thrashed and odd, almost futile but not broken. In need of straightening. Even broken, able to be reconnoitered and smoked. Maybe without a filter. And definitely with an end, a finality. Things are maybe not so hard as they seem. Less futile than he'd thought. There will be a tomorrow, with or without him,

Special thanks to my parents
and Kailyn Sciberras.
I love you.

If you think you're an addict, or might be, or definitely are, find a person place or thing to help. There's no right way to do it. Just try and put yourself with some right people and do what you can and can't do. Forgive yourself. And stop making your life harder. Try to love something or someone, even if it's just you.

ABOUT THE AUTHOR

Basic
Mutant
Psychosis:
Annals of
Los Angeles
2014-2016

Copyrighted Material
Cosmic Robotics
Morgan Drolet
&
Shawn Sullivan